Praise for Neil Smith's

BANG CRUNCH

NEIL SMITH
BANG CRUNCH

Neil Smith is a Montreal writer. He has won an honorable mention at the Canadian National Magazine Awards, first-prize at the Eden Mills Writers' Festival, and was nominated for the Journey Prize three times.

BANG
CRUNCH

STORIES

NEIL SMITH

Vintage Contemporaries
Vintage Books
A Division of Random House, Inc.
New York

FIRST VINTAGE CONTEMPORARIES EDITION, JANUARY 2008

Grateful acknowledgment is made to the following to reprint previously published material:

Edward Gorey Charitable Trust: Excerpt from *The Gashlycrumb Tinies* by Edward Gorey. Reprinted by permission of the Edward Gorey Charitable Trust.

Jane Siberry and Wing-It Music: "The Walking (and Constantly)," words and music by Jane Siberry. Copyright © 1987 Wing-It Music. Administered by Bug Music. Reprinted by permission of Jane Siberry and Wing-It Music.

The Library of Congress has cataloged the Knopf Canada edition as follows:
Smith, Neil, 1964–
Bang crunch / Neil Smith.
I. Title.
PS8637.M5655B35 2007
C813.'6
C2006 9012346-2

Vintage ISBN: 978-0-307-38610-6

www.vintagebooks.com

Printed in the United States of America
10   9   8   7   6   5   4   3   2   1

To Christian Dorais

I tell everyone a different story
that way nothing's ever boring
even when they turn and say you lied

JANE SIBERRY, "The Walking (and Constantly)"

CONTENTS

BANG CRUNCH

ISOLETTES

BLUE TUBE, GREEN TUBE, clear tube, fat tube. A Dr. Seuss rhyme. The tubes run from robotic Magi gathered around the incubator, snake through portholes in the clear plastic box, then burrow into the baby's pinkish grey skin. One tube up her left nostril. One tube down her throat. One tube into an arm no wider than a Popsicle stick. One tube tunnels into her chest. The skin of her chest is so thin. The baby's mother can almost see the tiny organs beneath, the way shrimp is visible under the rice paper of a spring roll. The baby doesn't move. Doesn't cry. To the mother, the baby, with its blue-black eyes, is an extraterrestrial crash-landed on her planet. Hidden away and kept alive by G-men while they assess what threat this tiny alien might pose.

"What kind of mother will you be?" Jacob asked. He and An sat side by side on a braided rug watching a flickering candle on An's coffee table. An said, "I won't be a mommy who bores people with the trials and tribulations of teething." Jacob disagreed: "You'll be like those TV-commercial moms who fret over whether to buy two-ply or three-ply toilet paper." From the coffee table, An picked up a blue ceramic cup, the kind used for espresso, and handed it to Jacob. "Real traditional," she said. "Real Norman Rockwell." Jacob grinned and stood, stretching his long legs. While he was in the bathroom, An got up and dropped a jazz CD in her player. Then she went into her bedroom and lay on her bed. Before the first song ended, Jacob came out of the bathroom. "You were fast this time," An said. Jacob replied that he'd been practising at home. He handed her the espresso cup and kissed her forehead. "I don't love you," he said. An replied, "I don't love you, too." After he'd let himself out of the apartment, An drew Jacob's semen into a syringe. She hiked up her peasant skirt and slid off her underwear. Then she lay on her bed, two pillows propped beneath her rear. It was the first time with the pillows: gravity, she reasoned, would help.

Neonatal Intensive Care Unit. Otherwise known as NICU. The doctors pronounce it NICK U, as if it were a university. "Our kid is studying at NICK U," Jacob jokes with a nurse, who stares at him blankly. An thinks of NICK U as a baby hatchery, one that smells like the stuff dentists use to clean teeth. The incubators, a dozen aquariums, are not in neat rows, but here and there, the way progressive schoolteachers arrange desks. Ventilators hum, monitors flash, alarms sound, a baby makes a noise like a gobbling turkey. Meanwhile, neonatologists complete their rounds. Some spill a hot alphabet soup of acronyms–ROP, BPD, C-PAP–in An's lap. Others say, with a hand on her shoulder, "We realize how stressful this must be." To them all, An wants to yell: "Nick you!" Better yet: "Nick off and die!"

Four months into An's pregnancy, Jacob moved into a top-floor apartment in her building. He called the place the *pent-up* suite because, according to An, the former tenants, a sulky husband and wife, were passive-aggressives. To exorcise the couple's demons, Jacob wandered around his stacks of moving boxes spritzing a citrus deodorizer. "If marriage is an institution," he said, "married people should be institutionalized." An wondered if this was a veiled reminder: that she and Jacob were not a couple, that they weren't bookends propping up *Dr. Spock's Baby and Childcare*. Still, the move into her building had been Jacob's idea. An concurred, though. Proximity without intimacy: it sounded good to her. She had no desire to actually live with Jacob or any other man. Men's bathroom habits, the Q-tips caked with earwax they left on the sink, depressed her. In her foolish twenties, she'd shared a loft with a boyfriend whose puppy-dog good cheer had made her want to drive him out into the country and leave him there. "Maybe more marriages would last if couples didn't live together," she said to Jacob as he unpacked a food processor the size of a space probe. "Maybe couples should buy two semi-detacheds and each live on either side," she added. Jacob laughed his nose-honking laugh. "That's why you always strike out at love, An," he said. "You're so semi-detached."

Between the twenty-third and twenty-fourth week of An's pregnancy, the placenta began to separate from the uterine wall. Semi-detached, An thought, when the doctor told her. By this time, she was lying under a spotlight in the emergency ward of the Royal Victoria Hospital. Her contractions were a minute apart. A nurse, the one who'd injected her with antibiotics earlier, yelled out, "Cervix fully effaced!" The warm amniotic fluid trickled over An's thighs, and the obstetrician soon announced, "She's crowning," as if An herself were Queen Victoria. Then came the huge, irresistible urge to push. When the neonatologist lifted her newborn daughter, An saw the tiny infant bat the air with one arm as if to clear everyone away, the doctors, the nurses—even her exhausted, terrified mother.

Though An hadn't wanted a baby shower, Jacob gave her one anyway. The theme, fittingly, was showers. The weather co-operated by drizzling. First, they took in the stage musical *Les parapluies de Cherbourg,* co-starring An's mother, Lise, who played an umbrella-shop owner in Normandy who meddled in her daughter's affair with a kind-hearted mechanic. The daughter got pregnant by the mechanic but ended up marrying a diamond importer she didn't love but grew to respect. During the standing ovation, Jacob whispered, "Only the French can make a *comédie musicale* depressing." Backstage, Lise pulled An into her dressing room and shut the door. Her stage makeup was as cracked as a Rembrandt. Lise sat at her vanity, pulled bobby pins from her soufflé of a wig and talked to An's reflection about the play's theme. "Not only passion and true love, but more subtle kinds of love and devotion and attachment." She talked loudly, as if she were still onstage. "You want me to marry a diamond importer?" An joked. Lise tossed her wig at An. "What I'm saying is, I'm trying to understand." An thanked her mother for making an effort—an effort that deflated when An opened the dressing-room door. In the hall, Jacob was talking to the mechanic, his hand on the actor's thigh. "Watch out for that one," Lise yelled to the mechanic. "He'll ejaculate into anything."

"What's your baby's name, honey?" the big woman asks. She has crinkly permed hair and fleshy upper arms. "Haven't thought of one yet," An mumbles. The woman sits beside An in the lounge outside NICK U. The chair creaks under her weight. Sheila delivered a twenty-nine-weeker. "We wanted to call our son Alek," she explains, "but he was born all pink and mewing and tiny like a newborn kangaroo, so we named him Joey." An has seen the sign taped to his incubator: HI, EVERYONE, MY NAME'S JOEY. Many of the incubators are personalized with signs. You can even stick stuffed animals through an incubator's porthole the way you'd place a treasure chest at the bottom of a fish tank. An tells Sheila she's afraid to name her baby, that naming her might be a jinx. An is surprised at herself: for saying such a thing (she's not superstitious) and for revealing something to a stranger. It must be exhaustion, or too many peanut butter cups from the vending machine. Sheila grabs An's hand and squeezes. "No, no, no," she insists. "Naming your baby will encourage her to live." Above Sheila's head is a poster of a baker frosting a cake with the letter B. The pattycake, pattycake man. "What about B?" An says. "Bea!" Sheila squeals and then adds, "Short for Beatrice. Like Beatrix Potter—nothing bad ever happens in Beatrix Potter!"

An's own name started as Anne Brouillette-Kappelhoff, the last name a coupling of her French-Canadian mother's and her German father's. When Anne was in high school, she often signed her papers Anne B-K to rein in her unwieldy name. By the time she hit university, she'd also sliced two letters off her first name. "A-N," she'd spell. "Like the indefinite article." It got people's attention. Made them think her eccentric, and at twenty-one, looking fourteen, that's what she wanted. While her friends dressed in black, she wore flowery Laura Ashley dresses, accented with green Doc Martens lace-up boots. In her creative writing class, she handed in "Gee, Your Hair Smells Terrific," a story about a crazed Avon lady who drowned a suburban housewife in a bubble bath. A boy in the class, who wore a spiked dog collar and an alligator polo shirt, liked the story very much. It was different, he said, from the "ethereal, lyrical, namby-pamby schlock" that the other girls handed in. The other girls began to hate this boy, whose name was Jacob.

Jacob sings "Supercalifragilisticexpialidocious" to B because he says she's so precocious. He waves to his four-day-old daughter through the plastic. She's the length of his forearm and weighs 520 grams, about the weight of the two sweet potatoes An bought for supper last night. Every day B gains the weight of a penny. "She's got your wrinkly forehead," Jacob says to An, who sits in a moulded plastic chair next to the incubator, smoothing out the yellow robe all the parents wear and twiddling the plastic bracelet that reads MOTHER 87308. Across from them, Sheila sits with her robe open and her blouse lifted. Joey, who's now two months old, cuddles against her stomach, the skin-to-skin contact that older preemies are allowed and that the nurses call "kangaroo care." Sheila is humming "You Are the Sunshine of My Life" because Stevie Wonder was a preemie. Jacob wanders over. "What bushy eyebrows you've got, little Joe. You're a dead ringer for Joseph Stalin." Sheila replies, "Are you calling my kid a communist?" Soon she has Jacob sitting in her seat with his shirt unbuttoned and Joey pressed against his chest. "You're no communist despot," Jacob murmurs to the baby, who's clad only in a diaper. "You're a little turnip head. A wobbly Weeble." Sheila tells Jacob that her husband holds Joey as comfortably as he would a purse. "But you, sir," she says, "are a natural." An listens to the two of them extol the virtues of kangarooing till she can take it no longer. She goes out the door of NICK.U and into the elevator and down to the lobby and out the front door. A pregnant woman is waddling in. Little head, huge belly, like an upside-down question mark: ¿. A single sob jumps from An's throat, and the woman throws her a startled look. An goes over to the bike rack in the hospital's parking lot and sits on a purple ten-speed with a banana seat. It's not hers, but it looks like the bike she had as a kid. It's a spring day, sunny but chilly. She breathes slowly and deeply through her nose as in her yoga class. After a half-hour, she feels almost serene. She goes back up to NICK U, where FATHER 87308 has become a thespian. "To B or not to B," he drones to his daughter.

———

Onstage was a stripper dressed in a fireman's yellow coat and rubber boots. The costume made dancing difficult, but he tried, shuffling back and forth to a rap song whose refrain went: "Don't blame me if your mental age is three." An's librarian friend Catou screwed up her face and said, "How could you have agreed to this?" She meant Part II of An's shower, which was held in a strip club called Wet. In the middle of the stage was a see-through shower stall where the fireman, now naked, was soaping his chest as water drizzled over him. Jacob had reserved a spot to one side of the stage. There, gathered around two tables pushed together, were eight of An's friends, a couple of translators and a few academics from the university where Jacob taught Russian lit. In the middle of the table was a stack of baby gifts: teething rings, pyjamas with the feet in, a duckie mobile. Jacob held his gift over his head: a clown doll the size of a ventriloquist's dummy with a bulbous nose and a wreath of rainbow hair. Mr. Pinkelton was his name. Jacob pressed the doll's belly, and Mr. Pinkelton emitted a phlegmy smoker's hack. "Only Jacob would buy a gift that could scare a baby to death," An said. Catou told An she had met a real clown that week, a social worker who dressed as Bozo to read to children at the library. "He's single and he loves kids," Catou said. "I could set you up."

An replied, "I'm six months pregnant, for Christ's sake." Up onstage, the stripper wagged his genitals like a clown twisting a dachshund out of party balloons.

When An had agreed to Catou's blind dates in the past, she would often see something in the man's eyes. Not passion, but more a yearning for passion. She, however, could never drum up the same enthusiasm. The whole dating scene always smacked of play-acting, like those histrionic *téléromans* her mother starred in. Her mother once set her up with a melodramatic actor named André, whom she dated for a few months. He was always haranguing her about the time she spent by herself. At an art gallery opening, he went into conniptions after finding her alone in the back alley petting a stray cat. "Are you some kind of Greta Garbo?" he raged. "Greta Garbage," she said because she'd been picking through a trash can for tidbits to feed the cat. When she and André broke up, she told Jacob she'd given up on relationships. Jacob insisted she'd never really given *in* to them. He likened her to a two-cigarette-a-day smoker who'd kicked the habit.

One blind date, a Korean immigrant still struggling with idiom, asked An, "What do you do for the living?"

With a stranger, small talk often kicks off with your job. So that's where An begins when she eventually leans over the incubator to introduce herself to B. "My name's An, and I'm a translator," she whispers. She admits to B that she'd always hoped to work at something creative. "Drawing, writing, acting—I have a little talent," she says. "But sometimes no talent is better. That way, you don't even try. When you have a little talent, you plough ahead regardless and get disappointed when you come up short." She explains that, in university, she'd first majored in English lit. But the professors were so fiercely intelligent that their IQs left scratch marks on her ego, so she switched over to translation. She now works freelance from home, mostly subtitling television documentaries. In her job, she shrinks people's words down to a pithy sentence that fits on the screen. "But B, who am I to put words in their mouths," she whispers, "when most of the time, I barely understand what *I'm* trying to say?" Across the room, Sheila spies An talking to B and gives a thumbs-up. Translation: Finally!

An can't help but like Sheila. The woman raises goldendoodles, a mix of golden retriever and poodle, in a backyard kennel she calls Doodsville. She shows An photos of the kennel and the dogs and then tapes a photo of her suburban bungalow to Joey's incubator, picture side against the plastic. "So he'll feel at home," she tells An. To her skinny marsupial baby, she promises, "Someday you'll have your father's beer belly and my fat ass." Like the neonatologists, she makes her rounds, visiting the other parents, asking questions. In the Pattycake Lounge (as An has dubbed it), she calls Jacob An's "hubby." And so An explains. Sheila's eyes grow even rounder behind her fishbowl glasses. A father who is sitting nearby and who calls the mother of his child "the wife" mutters, "That doesn't sound very natural." An is too weary to argue, but not Sheila. She gets up and throws open the door to NICK U, exposing the battery of machines keeping their children alive. "Show me one thing in there that's natural!"

Natural air is twenty-one-percent oxygen. That's what Dr. Amelios, the neonatologist, is telling An and Jacob. B lies in her incubator, a tiny stocking cap wiggled onto her head to help conserve body heat. The clear tube down her throat is her air tube. B wrenches her head sideways as if to free herself. "This baby is state-of-the-art," Dr. Amelios says, and until he pats a hand against the ventilator contraption, An thinks he's referring to B. "It oscillates fast, so it does little damage to the lungs," he says. An says, "Little damage?" The doctor explains that oxygen is dangerous for preemies, given their underdeveloped lungs. Too much oxygen can dilate the blood vessels, detach retinas. An says, a bit impatiently, "I've always suspected oxygen of getting off easy. Sure, we blame greenhouse gases, but maybe it's the oxygen killing us all." Dr. Amelios looks perplexed. Jacob looks embarrassed. For the third time in three days, Jacob says, "An, it's not your fault." She snaps, "I never thought it was." But this is a lie. Months ago, she'd told the truth when Jacob asked why she wanted a baby. She felt a bit adrift, she'd said. Bringing up a child would anchor her. Now she feels she's dropped that anchor overboard without securing it to the boat.

At twenty-four weeks, a newborn's chances of survival are seventy percent. Severe disabilities occur at a rate of twenty percent. At twenty-three weeks, survival drops to forty percent and disabilities jump to sixty. An tries memorizing these figures the way she once studied for math tests. She thinks: Which is older? A baby born at twenty-three weeks who's lived two and a half weeks out of the womb? Or a baby delivered three days ago at twenty-five weeks? Sitting in her plastic chair, she watches a nurse spread Vaseline goo on a baby's skin to keep it moist. Across from An,

Joey is being fitted with a breathing apparatus that resembles scuba gear. It's called a C-PAP. What do the letters stand for? Concentrate, she orders herself. Just figure out this fucking acronym and everything will be fine. She feels nauseated, woozy. She leans over and crosses her arms under her knees, the position to assume in an emergency landing. Her head is so heavy, her skull a playpen strewn with the new words she's learned. Extremely premature babies are micro-preemies. The incubators are called isolettes. Then there's the whole litany of words for what can go wrong: bradycardia, apnea, bronchopulmonary dysplasia, desatting, spastic diplegia, tracheotomy, retinopathy of prematurity.

Jacob brings An a *caffe latte* from a nearby coffee shop. With her hands wrapped around the warm Styrofoam cup, she mutters, "I don't want this." Jacob replies that it's decaf. "The bells and whistles, the tubes, the deadly oxygen," An says. "I don't want any of this." Jacob sighs, looks up at the fluorescent lights, looks down at B, who's wearing a mask over her eyes, like those that flight attendants hand out to passengers. Jacob mumbles, "She'll die without them." An says calmly, "If my womb rejected her, maybe she was meant to." She doesn't look at Jacob or B but instead examines the sprinkle of cinnamon atop her coffee. She feels Jacob's stare. "You're tired, An," he says. "You don't want to make rash decisions when you're tired." Listen to him. So adult, so un-Jacob. What would he do if she unplugged the machines, unhooked the tubes and let their baby be? Euthanasia. As a child, she'd thought people were saying "youth in Asia." She'd pictured newborn Chinese girls swaddled in blankets and left on mountainsides to die.

An's mother is entertaining the troops. That's how An sees it. Lise is standing in the middle of NICK U with the other parents crowded around. They recognized her, of course. Her presence here is lucky, they must think. In the seventies, Lise played the Black Mouse in the children's television show *Les souris dansent.* The part became her bête noire because, when the show ended, she struggled to get acting jobs in programs for adults. Lise is telling the parents about a miscarriage she had in her late thirties. An, her two younger sisters and her parents had been driving through Chicoutimi when her mother started bleeding. "After I lost the baby, I couldn't stop crying," Lise says. "The nurse wheeled me back to the waiting room, took a look at my three little girls and said, 'Why all the fuss? You don't have enough kids as it is?'" The parents tsk-tsk, and Sheila touches Lise's arm in commiseration. An recalls that, when her mother was pregnant, she'd flick the heads of dandelions into An's face and say, "Mommy had a baby and her head popped off." Now An looks at her mother, wet-eyed and basking in the attention. She was a good mother, An thinks. She really was. Though at times, when Lise played with An and her sisters, dressed them all up in wigs and costumes for Little Red Riding Hood or Heidi, An had the uneasy feeling her mother was rehearsing for a part.

The blue espresso cup, the one Jacob had masturbated into, sat on the concrete wall of An's balcony. By this time, An was two months pregnant, already spitting up every morning in the kitchen sink. Jacob decided that, for luck, they had to break the cup. Toss it ten storeys to smash in the parking lot below. They were talking about parenthood, and Jacob was describing his own parents, who lived out west. His father was a constant complainer, prone to tantrums. When he'd discovered Jacob's stash of stolen Barbie dolls, he'd taken them to his tool shed and decapitated them. "I remember screaming at him to at least spare the black one. She was unique—she was Afro Barbie." An mentioned her own parents, how her father and mother were so much in love they still took bubble baths together, with scented candles atop the toilet tank. Jacob joked, "Their profound love has set expectations that no boyfriend of yours can match." An replied, "Thank you, Dr. Kitchensink" and then pushed the blue cup off the edge.

An is telling B about Jacob. She talks about his feigned cynicism, his pretence at unconventionality with his dyed blue-black hair, the lizard tattooed on his hipbone. He's threatened to spike the lounge's water cooler with ecstasy. Play some trance music over the PA system. A rave in NICK U! Strung-out fathers unfrazzled. Moms dancing with their kid's ventilator. "But really, B, Jacob is more dewy-eyed than my sisters and girlfriends. On an errand to pick up his dry cleaning, he'll fall in love twice." The unconventional one, An admits, is herself. "I don't fall in love, but I do fall in *like*. I could probably fall deeply in like." She looks at B's face, distorted by the air tube jammed into her mouth. She recalls Jacob kidding with her mother, asking why the French language doesn't distinguish between like and love. Why *aimer* is enough. Lise said that, for French people, to like is to love. "What do you think, B?" An asks her baby. She sticks a hand through the porthole and, with her index finger, touches B's elbow.

———

When An opens the front door to her apartment, she still smells taupe. That's the colour she painted her bedroom two weeks earlier. In the entrance hall are the bags of baby-shower gifts she got the night her contractions started. Sticking out the top of one bag is Mr. Pinkelton's malicious clown face. Her fantasy of tossing the gifts down the garbage chute is interrupted by the phone. She doesn't answer. All week she's been talking to friends and family, repeating to everyone her Cole Porter refrain: "It's just one of those things." On her balcony, she pops open a bottle of Cabernet Sauvignon, thinking that at least now she can drink. As she sips, she sees the greenhouses atop McGill University's agriculture building a few blocks away. All that greenery so far off the ground is miraculous and consoling. In the apartment tower kitty-corner from hers, a woman carries a chair onto her balcony and steps onto it. For a dizzying instant, An thinks she's going to jump, but the woman simply hangs a pot of ivy.

An walks back to the hospital. The sun beats hot on her head. She's still dabbing sweat from her forehead as she enters the Pattycake Lounge. There, Sheila lurches out of her seat and flings herself at An. An feels the drag of the woman's weight, her body heat;

she smells the oiliness of Sheila's scalp. Sheila begins sobbing, the sound resembling Mr. Pinkelton's phlegmy cough. An tries to pat the woman's back and pull away at the same time. "Joey?" An asks.

Jacob is in a private room down the hall from NICK U, in a plastic chair, cradling B in a tiny handmade quilt of green and yellow squares. Only B's face is visible. An sees that, without the air tube, the baby's mouth has the same rosebud lips as Jacob. He is singing now. Softly, slowly, as if his song were a lullaby, singing about the longest word he's ever heard. She chose him as the father, thinking he wouldn't get attached. Yet here he is—cradling and crooning to his daughter. An sits on a trundle bed next to him. She fingers the quilt. The hospital gives these to parents as mementos: quilts and locks of hair and footprints of their dead babies. She wonders if, under the quilt, B's feet are already black with ink. Jacob says, "Would you like to hold her?" But An simply touches B's head, the soft spot where you can feel a baby's heartbeat but where she feels nothing. Jacob resumes his song, almost in a whisper now. An stares at B in his arms; she recalls the baby pushing everyone away in the delivery room. After a moment, she says, "I don't love you." She waits for Jacob's usual "I don't love you, too," but when he looks at her, his face is ashen. He has understood what she meant. "Why?" he says, with a look of pain and puzzlement. "Oh, but I liked her," An says, almost pleadingly. "I liked her so much." Jacob starts crying. Soundlessly. When he finishes, he murmurs, "Well, that's something." And An, her arms wrapped around herself, holding herself together, hopes that it is.

GREEN FLUORESCENT PROTEIN

THE HUMAN GENOME is what Ruby-Doo is babbling about. The two of us are in Westmount Park. I'm practising my hook shots as he slumps on a bench alongside the basketball court.

Ruby-Doo has, what else, a book in his hands. He's a shortish, skinnyish guy. Well, at least compared with me.

"Wouldn't it be incredible," he says, scratching his armpit, "to map the thousands of genes in your body? Track down where each one comes from. Discover hidden traits."

Yesterday, his mother told me Ruby-Doo is a gifted child. But isn't gifted *child* an insult at seventeen? I'm seventeen too. One of my biggest gifts: twirling a b-ball on my index finger.

I sink the ball from half-court, and Ruby-Doo does the fake crowd roar—the hushed wahhhh—I taught him. I dribble over to his bench.

"Say you harbour the gene to become a musical prodigy," he says, blinking in the July sun. "Except you're totally unaware because you've never sat down at a piano. Unlike dwarfism or red hair, musical genius isn't visible. You see it only under special conditions."

In a field beside the courts, a theatre troupe is rehearsing *Romeo and Juliet*. Every now and then, Ruby-Doo is drowned out by some goof in tights yelling "Prodigious birth of love it is to me!" or something equally lame. But Ruby-Doo doesn't seem to notice; he rattles on about certain genes being top-secret files we need special security clearance to open. I remember my mom saying that alcoholism is hereditary and that maybe she and I both have the gene, so I tell Ruby-Doo I don't want to open those secret files.

"Probably bad news," I say.

Ruby-Doo eyes me like he's working on a science report on today's average teenager. "You know, Hippie," he says, "sometimes you're a real naysayer."

What the hell's a naysayer?

"Piss off," I say.

My real name is Max. Hippie is what Ruby-Doo calls me. The nickname is a joke: I have a buzz cut, wear polo shirts with little alligator logos and play on a basketball team. I call René-Louis Robidoux by his last name, pronouncing it like Scooby-Doo. We met at the start of the summer, when my mom and I moved to Westmount from Saint-Bruno.

Every afternoon while I was shooting baskets, Ruby-Doo would be in the park reading. He always looked so absorbed; it bugged me. One day, I deliberately shot the ball at him, sending his book flying.

Apologizing, I went and picked up the book and dusted it off. On the cover was the whiskered mug of a monkey. "What's your book about?" I asked, handing it over.

The Third Chimpanzee, he said, was about evolution and genetics, about the development of language and art.

"And also about sexuality," he added.

"Sexuality?"

"Yeah, like why women can't tell when they're ovulating," he said, straight-faced. "Like why men have such long dicks but such small balls compared with chimps."

I held the b-ball to my hip. "You're kidding, right?"

His mouth curled into a grin. That's when I noticed his eyes: one was brownish, the other blue. Just like some Alaskan huskies you see.

My mom and I moved to Westmount as part of her Life Overhaul. She wanted everything new. New job: as a partner in a private dermatology clinic. New boyfriend: a dweeb anaesthesiologist named Brian who calls me Sport and sucks on toothpicks in public. New hair dye: something called Peruvian Fire (looks like the colour of barbecue chips). New AA group: the Westmount chapter, which she goes to every week.

Our new home is the top floor of this big brick house around the corner from the YMCA. The apartment has a wicked long hallway, like a bowling alley of blond wood. Another cool thing: the private bathroom off my bedroom has a fancy stained glass window that makes taking a leak a religious experience.

One night, I get home from Passion des Fruits—the grocery store where I stack produce part-time—and find my mom sprucing up for a date. She frowns at herself in a hallway mirror. "These canine teeth of mine," she says, "stick out like box seats at the opera."

While poking in her clunky earrings, she asks

whether Brian reminds me of my dad: "You know, the bear chest, the pointy chin."

"Maybe," I say. "Except Brian isn't some dead stiff whose widow is already screwing around."

My mom turns the colour of her hair. "You little shit," she spits out. "Don't you tell me how to grieve."

"Ma, I'm only joking," I lie.

She throws an earring at me. Misses me by a mile.

Two years ago, my dad died of a brain aneurysm. Just dropped dead on the curling rink while lining up a shot. He was a big curler, my dad. He once joked he'd like his ashes placed in a hollowed-out curling stone.

Guess what—my mom decided to do it.

"For cripe's sake, he was only kidding!" I shouted and then burst into these weird yelping sobs. My mom grabbed me by the shoulders, pressing so hard my tears instantly stopped. "Listen to me, Max," she said in a freaky yell-whisper. "We all need a little levity. You understand me?"

I didn't argue. I didn't want to stress her out even more, because in times of stress she might drop in on her old buddies Chardonnay and Sauvignon Blanc. Two weeks after the funeral, I found her in the kitchen, pale and shaky. In her hands was a two-arm corkscrew contraption, like something you'd abort a fetus with.

"Whatcha doing, Ma?" My voice sounded small and babyish. Scared.

"Nothing, honey," she mumbled.

That's when I saw the bottle of white wine on the counter. I stood in the doorway, watching her uncork her bottle, pour a glass and dump the rest—*clug, clug, clug*—down the sink. Then she held her glass up, stuck her nose inside . . . and just sniffed!

As she shuffled out of the kitchen, she handed me the glass of wine. I took a sip of the stuff—it tasted like liquid headache—and then poured the rest into a vase of wilting funeral flowers.

"Remarkable," Ruby-Doo says when he sees the curling stone sitting on my mom's desk like some mammoth paperweight.

"Can I pick it up?"

I nod, and he lifts the stone gently by its curved handle and sits with it in a leather armchair. He rubs his palm over the stone's granite surface, which is bluish grey with these flecks of white.

Till Ruby-Doo, I've told none of my friends about the curling stone: it's damn embarrassing when your dad's a cremated genie in a bottle.

"Tell me about your father," Ruby-Doo says.

So I sit down on my mom's bed and talk about my

dad. How he was an English lit prof at CEGEP. How in front of my friends he used expressions like "gee willickers" and "jiminy cricket" just to mortify me.

"Tell me more, Hippie," Ruby-Doo keeps saying. So I keep tripping down memory lane, dodging a few potholes, like how miserable my mom's drinking made my dad.

"His voice," I say, "was a real tw*aaangy* drawl 'cause he grew up in Alab*aaama*. And what a motormouth—he was always blabbing away. I'd fade him out like Muzak. But after he died, our house got dead quiet, so I guess I kind of missed the background noise of his voice."

I don't usually tell people super-confidential things like this. But I do with Ruby-Doo, and I swear he gets all teary-eyed. For a couple seconds, I feel the same awful pain I felt when my dad died—like having shin splints in your heart. But then I glance over at Ruby-Doo and burst out laughing.

"What?" he says. "What's so funny?"

The guy is cradling and petting the curling stone like a frigging pussycat. I take the stone from him and put it back on the desk. Then I pick Ruby-Doo up—he's as light as a girl—and throw him on my mom's bed.

"Hey," he says. "Hey!"

From the living room, my mom yells, "No rough-housing," like we're ten years old.

———

Ruby-Doo's house is big and dark and crammed with old, uncomfortable furniture with claw feet. On the walls are these gloomy sepia photographs of dead relatives.

He's invited me over for his parents' backyard barbecue. I'm expecting hot dogs and hamburgers, but the party is catered. Waiters carrying trays of dinky hors d'oeuvres snake through a crowd of guests. There are men in linen suits and bow ties. There's a woman hired to play violin. Apart from two six-year-old brats who keep winging a Frisbee at the violinist, I'm the youngest person here.

For some privacy, Ruby-Doo and I eat our dessert—sugar pie—on his screened-in veranda. He's jabbering on about this freakazoid named Nicholas Pop, an American artist who transfers genes between species.

"The guy has isolated the green fluorescent protein that makes the Pacific Northwest jellyfish glow," Ruby-Doo says, waving his fork. "And get this: he's injected that gene into the zygote of a guinea pig. Straight into its DNA."

His face lights up and his left knee jiggles as he talks. Watching him, I realize how bizarre my old Saint-Bruno friends would consider Ruby-Doo.

"Under regular light, the animal looks normal—just an albino guinea pig. But add some ultraviolet light, and the thing glows an eerie fluorescent green."

"Why call this quack an artist?" I ask. "Is a glow-in-the-dark rodent art?"

"Depends," Ruby-Doo mumbles, his mouth packed with pie. He swallows loudly. "What if art is finding beauty in unexpected places?"

This Pop guy has a website: www.chimera.com. Ruby-Doo emailed him a sort of fan letter and Pop replied. Seems Pop will be lecturing in Montreal soon and has sent Ruby-Doo two free tickets. Ruby-Doo pulls the tickets from his pocket and hands me one.

"For you, Hippie," he says, patting my knee. "To thank you for listening to my deranged rambling."

The ticket is fluorescent green. On one side is the date of the lecture, along with the address of the theatre. On the other side is one word, which I say out loud: "Glow."

Us eating out, my mom jokes, is how my dad would want his insurance money spent. So every Thursday night, we go to a new restaurant—Indian, Ethiopian, Thai, Mexican, whatever—and try ordering something we don't usually put in our mouths. Tonight, I polish off fava bean chowder and quail stuffed with apples and thyme; my mom downs escargot with goat cheese and then a bowl of oysters. We're in this homey

French place with a dozen tables. Ours is covered in a yellow tablecloth decorated in a pattern of sunflowers and what look like dung beetles.

While I check out the dessert menu, my mom asks how I'm enjoying my summer job.

"I stacked a tub of eggplants today," I say. "Ever notice how beautiful they are? With their little purple bellies like Buddha."

I'm trying to find beauty in unexpected places, but my mother just looks at me funny. "What's happened to my son, the Jock Philistine?" she says.

"The Jock Philistine" is what my old girlfriend, Madison O'Connor, used to call me. Even in front of my mom.

"Heard from Madison lately?" my mom asks, and I shake my head.

Madison wore perfume that smelled like that strawberry powder you mix in milk. After she moved to Chicago, I bought a can of the stuff to remember her by. But by the time I'd finished the can, we'd more or less stopped writing each other.

"Some relationships just fizzle out," my mom says and sighs real dramatically, like she's in a play.

"Okay—what's up?"

She plays origami with her napkin a bit. Then blurts out: "Brian proposed to me."

The quail I ate is suddenly pecking its way through my gut.

"I'm going to say no," she says, seeing my stunned look. "We've only been dating four months." She rummages her hands through her hair. "Brian is lovely, but he's . . . a tad boring. I mean, the man's the only anaesthesiologist who doesn't need drugs to put a person to sleep."

She laughs at her joke, her trademark guffaw that flashes the fillings in her teeth.

I feel guilty having hassled her about Brian. "You dating," I say, "I think it's a good thing."

My mom raises her eyebrows at me.

"No, I really do," I say and wonder if it's the truth. Then I say what I know is the truth: "Dad would want you to."

I feel sort of bad bringing my father up, but my mom just smiles down at her empty oyster shells, her bowl of castanets.

That night, I overhear my mom talking in her room with the door shut. She says, "One thousand days of sobriety." I assume she's on the phone with one of her batty friends, till she adds, "Can you believe it, Carl?"

She's talking to the curling stone.

————

On Friday, I have the day off from the grocery store. Around noon, our door buzzer buzzes. When I press the intercom, I hear Ruby-Doo's crackly voice whining, "Can Max come out and play?"

He takes me on a tour of some of his favourite sights in Montreal. Outside Square-Victoria metro station, he points out these street lamps: two curvy, lizard-green monstrosities with piss-yellow eyes. They're extraterrestrials attacking a suburban town in a horror flick from the fifties. In a nearby building, we ride his favourite elevator: a birdcage-like contraption operated by a dandruffy old geezer. All the way up, this guy announces the floors in a bilingual garble: "twauziemturdfloor . . . katriemfortfloor."

Later, we walk down a snaky street where cobblestones poke through the asphalt. Sandwiched between two brick triplexes is this tiny wooden house Ruby-Doo wants to show me. It's caramel-coloured and has big shutters and a shingled roof. If we rang the bell, the door would be answered by Hansel and Gretel.

Farther down the street is a little park with a cement statue of a curled-up dog taking a snooze. Ruby-Doo pats the dog's head and says, "What about you, Hippie? What sorts of things do you love?"

Nothing leaps to mind, so I say, "Taking walks with

my retarded friend," and Ruby-Doo beams me this
sunny smile like I've given him a supreme compliment.

Around suppertime, we wander through the downtown core. The streets are closed off for the jazz festival, and hundreds of people are milling around. A
stage is set up in front of the art museum. We find an
empty stretch of grass on the museum's lawn and
plunk ourselves down. Sitting nearby are two punks: a
purple-haired guy and a blue-haired girl, both with
shaved eyebrows. Ruby-Doo points out the pet rat
Blue Hair has perched on her shoulder. "You think
you're special, Hippie," he says. "But dismantle your
genome and you'll find you have the same building
blocks as that rat."

I'm about to say, *I don't think I'm special,* but stop
myself because the day has been one of those perfect
days that have you believing you *are* something special.

Ruby-Doo says the rat and I have been put together
with the same deluxe set of Lego. "What differs," he says,
"is the pieces chosen and the order they're stacked in."

Up onstage, a singer vacuum-packed into a tight
dress slinks over to the mike. I lie back in the grass
and listen to her low, gravely voice sing about love
and loss, and Ruby-Doo's high, cheery voice talk
about life and Lego.

———

We play two-on-one: me against Ruby-Doo and the nurse from *Romeo and Juliet*. The nurse's name is Charlotte, a pretty, twenty-year-old girl who probably didn't get cast as Juliet because she's black and fat.

"Get your skinny butt moving," she yells at Ruby-Doo, lobbing him the ball.

He looks at her in amazement. By the time Charlotte is called back to rehearsal, Ruby-Doo's T-shirt is spotted with sweat, like those ink-blot tests shrinks use. He falls down on the court. "No more," he huffs. "God have mercy on my skinny white butt."

We head back to my place to eat supper and watch his favourite movie, *2001: A Space Odyssey*. My mom is in the kitchen, stirring a wooden spoon in a pot on the stove. "*Salut*, Max. *Salut*, Ruby-Doo," she says. "*Je vous fais du chili ce soir, les gars.*"

This bugs me for two reasons. First, only I get to call René-Louis Ruby-Doo. Second, why does my mom always humiliate me with her crappy French?

My mom scoops out some chili and holds the spoon to Ruby-Doo's lips. "*Délicieux,*" he mumbles. Some sauce has smudged on his chin, and my mom wipes it off with a dish towel, slinging an arm across his shoulder. Then she ruffles his hair. My mom has always been touchy-feely, which can be mortifyingly embarrassing.

Ruby-Doo looks at her shyly. "Want to watch the movie with us, Peggy?"

Peggy says she can't because she's leaving in five minutes for AA.

Peggy says AA like it was PTA.

Ruby-Doo looks a bit flustered. "Oh, okay," he says. "Hey, I'm sorry."

"No need to be," my mom insists. "My drinking has been under control for years." Then: "You're surprised because I'm a doctor."

"No, no," he says.

"Some MDs even drink on the job," my mom says. "The oath they take is hypocritical rather than Hippocratic." She does her usual guffaw.

As I pour us glasses of water, Ruby-Doo says in his Mr. Science mode that he's read alcoholism is a disease.

More like a self-inflicted wound, I think. My mom once picked me up from Cub Scouts totally plastered. After that, the scout leader always asked how my "home life" was, like he was all eager to call Children's Aid.

As my mom natters on, I announce that Ruby-Doo has to take his shower. Once he's gone off to my room, my mom turns to me: "Does my alcoholism still embarrass you?" She jabs her wooden spoon at me. "I've learned to accept it, and so should you."

Sounds like step eight of her twelve-step program.

"Look, what embarrasses me," I say, "is you pawing Ruby-Doo." To be nasty, I add, "Aren't you too old for him?"

She looks at me and laughs.

"You slay me, kid," she says.

After my mom is gone, I peel off my sweaty T-shirt and push open the door to my room. Puddly footprints trail from my bathroom to my dresser. Ruby-Doo stands at the dresser mirror, raking a comb across his head. At his feet is his duffel bag, with a tumble of clothes hanging out.

I walk up behind him. One of my beach towels circles his waist, and water beads on his back. On the nape of his neck are these little blond hairs.

"So is skinny-ass all clean?" I say. As a joke, I yank his towel off. I'm going to say, *Yep, sure is skinny,* but with him there naked, the words get trapped behind my teeth.

In the mirror, Ruby-Doo is watching me, his pupils the size of pennies. We stare at each other like it's a staring contest, so I feel like the loser when I blink and look away.

He lays his comb down and turns slowly around. I see his blue eye first, then his brown eye. He reaches up, cups a hand around my left biceps.

He squeezes.

I pull away.

"Shower time," I mumble. I hurry into the bathroom, locking the door.

The shower I take is long and cool, but somehow I'm still sweating after I switch off the taps.

During the opening scene, an ape-man swings a club and crushes the skull of a wild boar.

On opposite ends of the couch, Ruby-Doo and I sit watching *2001*. His voice cracking like a thirteen-year-old puberty case, Ruby-Doo says, "It's good your mom goes to AA."

I say, "Uh-huh." I keep my eyes glued to the TV screen and spoon chili into my mouth.

In another scene, a spacecraft flies to the moon. On board is a stewardess who wears shoes with Velcro soles to anchor her to the floor.

Later, when Ruby-Doo finally leaves, I walk around our apartment like that stewardess. Taking careful, measured steps so I don't float off into zero gravity.

For the next few days, Ruby-Doo is in Quebec City, attending his older sister's wedding. I stack Swiss chard and bok choy; I stack tangerines and mangoes.

I call up Pete, an old friend from Saint-Bruno, and

we go skating on the bike paths that criss-cross the Plateau. Pete is tall and gangly; he has red hair and a smattering of freckles. With Rollerblades on, he's a giraffe on wheels.

We buy hot dogs blanketed in sauerkraut and wolf them down sitting on a stoop outside a french-fry place. Pete nudges me and nods toward two girls sitting nearby. He whispers, "Eager beavers," his expression for girls on the make.

I look over at the girls. Then I look past them, down a back lane where every duplex has an outdoor spiral staircase twisting from the ground to the top balcony.

During our walking tour, Ruby-Doo compared Montreal's spiral staircases to DNA.

I wonder what he's doing at this exact moment. What he's thinking about. Then I realize it's damn faggy to wonder these things and that I'd better snap out of it.

So I go talk to the girls with Pete. I make jokes. I flash a big cheesy smile. To show off, I do a hand-stand with my skates on. With my T-shirt riding up, the blood pooling in my head, the hot dog somer-saulting in my stomach, I almost feel normal.

Last year, I was at this party thrown by this guy Charlie Deller, a basketball player from another school. At one point, Charlie took me into his dad's study. At the wet bar, he poured us glasses of crème de menthe, which tastes like concentrated mouthwash. Charlie was a little drunk. One minute he was bragging about bench-pressing one-eighty; next minute he leaned over and licked my cheek like it was a frigging ice cream cone. "You've got nice skin," he said just before his girlfriend walked in.

A week later, our b-ball team played his. Charlie Deller saw me, said, "Hey, man, how's it going?" All nonchalant, like it wasn't queer for people to go around licking faces.

Charlie decided to ignore what had happened. Pretty smart move, because now, whenever I bump into him, I practically think I dreamed the whole cheek-licking episode up.

Saturday afternoon, I'm in the park, slam-dunking a few, when Ruby-Doo rides up on his clunky bicycle, a knapsack strapped to his back. I go over to say hi, hugging the b-ball to my stomach; I ask how the wedding was.

"Stuffy. Overblown," he says. "I'm never getting married."

Ruby-Doo smiles, and I feel creepy, like maybe him never having a wife has a hidden meaning. So I look down at a little sandy anthill spilling out of a crack in the concrete. I smudge the anthill with my foot.

Ruby-Doo opens the drawstring of his knapsack and yanks out a big box wrapped in aluminum foil. "For you," he says, handing it over.

I stand there staring at the box, my throat as dry as a tortilla chip.

"Well, go ahead and open it." He rubs his palms on his jeans like he's wiping away sweat.

I unpeel the foil. It's a shoebox. Inside are Riko basketball sneakers. Fire hydrant red stripes and air-bubble soles. Tongues sticking out at me.

"It's not my birthday."

"So what?" Ruby-Doo says. "Try them on. You take nine and a half, right?"

I sit on the bench, wriggle my old sneakers off and lace the Rikos up. Then I boing up and down the court, thinking, So he bought you a gift. Means nothing.

"Perfect fit," I say.

"Look at you," Ruby-Doo shouts with a big smile. "Cinderella of the basketball court."

I glare at him: "What'd you call me?"

"What?" he says.

In the pissed-off yell-whisper my mom uses on me, I snap, "I'm no Cinderella, okay?"

"Okay, okay," Ruby-Doo replies. Then a sly look flits across his face. "But you got to admit," he says, "when it comes to princes, I'm pretty charming."

My anger stings like a rug burn.

I rip the left Riko off and throw it on the ground. The right Riko I whip across the court at Ruby-Doo's head, smacking him hard in the face.

He flinches. Cups a hand over his nose.

I just stand there, embarrassed. Like a ten-year-old who's had a tantrum in public.

Ruby-Doo draws his hand away. I expect blood, but there's none. Still, his nose is blotchy and his eyes are red and teary.

He walks toward me.

I look down at my stocking feet; I expect him to punch me, and I hope he does. But he brushes past, his shoulder skimming mine. Under his breath, he mutters, "You're welcome."

When I get home, I shove the Rikos under my bed with my old puzzles and dinosaur models and sports trophies.

Nauseous and dizzy—that's how I feel. Like my organs—heart, stomach, pituitary gland—are strapped into a Rotowhirl at the midway.

I lie on my bed.

I try to think. I try to stay calm. I try to be logical.

Okay, proof I'm not queer: I did it with Madison once. So what if it wasn't that romantic? We'd had a bath together first, and she'd poured in tons of bubble-bath powder. Well, the stuff left a gross soapy film on our skin. Still, all my parts worked the way they're supposed to. The whole time I kept thinking we were performing some weird calisthenics for gym class.

I think, Do I want to do calisthenics with Ruby-Doo?

Then I feel totally disgusted. At myself for hurting Ruby-Doo. At Ruby-Doo for calling me his princess.

And especially at myself for wanting to hold Ruby-Doo after I hurt him.

Later there's a knock on my bedroom door.

"Go away!" I yell at my mom.

She comes in anyway, spritzing her neck with eau de toilette and wearing a blouse that looks like the stuff they make doilies out of. She flushed Brian last week and already has a coffee date with some chatroom conquest she met on the Internet.

"How do I look?"

I lie that she has too much lipstick on, and she kisses a Kleenex to blot her mouth.

"I hope you know," I say, "that women are entrapped on the Net and sold into white slavery."

Picking invisible lint from her skirt, she says, "Sometimes, Max, you've got to be willing to take such chances."

I want to say, *Don't go.* Not that I'm afraid her date is an axe murderer. Or that I don't want her meeting someone, getting over my father. Or even that I want to talk about what's eating me. I'd just like her here, that's all. Putzing around the apartment the way moms do, while I sulk in my room.

She bends down, kisses my forehead. "You still going out with René-Louis tonight?" she asks.

I shrug. That lecture with the damn glow-in-the-dark rodent is at seven o'clock. My green fluorescent ticket is thumbtacked to my bulletin board.

After my mom leaves, I pour myself some Cheerios for supper. But my appetite is shot, so I leave the little life preservers floating in their milk.

I pace around the apartment. Drift from room to room. I end up in my mom's room, flipping through *Romeo and Juliet,* which I spot on her bookshelf. It's my dad's classroom copy, all dog-eared and mangled. In the margins, he's pencilled in his comments.

"Love isn't a play on words," he's written in Act II. "Rather, it's words at play, let out at recess to go swing on the monkey bars."

What the fuck does that mean?

Suddenly, I'm furious at my dad for being so frigging cryptic, for not being here to set me straight. For being stone-cold dead.

I grab the curling stone and go into our bowling-alley hallway. I slide that sucker down the hall with such force it smacks against the back wall, nicking the paint and leaving a monster dent.

I sit on the floor.

I jab the tips of my index fingers into the corners of my eyes to stop myself from bawling.

It doesn't work.

Once, when I was thirteen, I saw my dad cry.

We were staying at our cottage on Danforth Lake. I'd been off picking raspberries. When I got back, I could hear my mom's voice: loud and gin-and-tonicky. She was on the patio with the German couple from the cottage next door.

When she saw me, she screeched, "There's my baby!"

To get away from her, I went down to the dock. My dad was sitting there, his feet dangling in the water. I snuck up, hoping to scare him. But before I could yell "Raahh!" the dock creaked and my dad turned his head.

His cheeks were wet, his eyes bloodshot. Snot was rolling out of his nose.

I was terrified.

Still, I sat down beside him, dunked my feet in the water and watched tadpoles as big as kiwi fruit nibble at my toes.

"You hate her, don't you?" I finally said. "You hate her guts."

"No, Max," he said, wiping the snot with the back of his hand. "I was crying because I love her guts."

It's seven-thirty by the time I reach Ex-Centris, the theatre where Nicholas Pop is giving his talk on glowing rodents. Out front, a dozen picketers are traipsing up and down the sidewalk. They wear green glow-in-the-dark necklaces and wave placards: BRILLER, C'EST PAS BRILLANT! and REMEMBER DR. FRANKENSTEIN!

The beefy guy at the door doesn't want to let me in, but when I whip out my ticket he sweeps me through. Ex-Centris is one long lobby with a stone floor and a glass ceiling. Off the lobby are three rooms. The ticket girl says I'm late and points me toward the Salle Fellini.

I slink inside this low-lit hall, where a guy dressed in black is onstage talking. Scanning the audience–there must be two hundred people here–I finally spot the back of Ruby-Doo's head near the front.

As I'm wedging into the second row, the guy onstage–Pop, I guess–says, "I don't care about aesthetics. Aesthetics to me is what primatology is to monkeys." The audience starts laughing; so does Ruby-Doo, till he sees me toddling toward him. After stepping my Rikos on seventeen feet, I shoehorn myself into the empty seat beside him.

"Hi," I whisper.

"Well, if it ain't Cinderella's ugly stepsister," he mutters, looking straight ahead.

"Yeah," I say.

There's a chalky taste, like a dissolved Aspirin, in my mouth. I turn and face the stage. That's when I notice the albino guinea pig. It's inside a see-through plastic hutch set on a table near Pop.

"Man has tinkered with the evolution of plants and animals for thousands of years. So creating hybrids violates no social precedence," Pop says, his voice booming through some hidden mike. The guy is a preacher with a rock star's goatee and leather pants. He talks on about jellyfish and mutation and enzymes while a screen behind him flashes images of petri dishes, X and Y chromosomes and whatnot.

I'm barely paying attention. Instead, I listen to Ruby-Doo's breath going in and out. Here's what you do, I think. Apologize. Tell him he's a great guy, a good friend—but just a friend. Then do a Charlie Deller and pretend nothing happened.

Pop fishes his guinea pig out of its hutch. Its hind

legs pirouette as the guy tucks the animal to his chest. We're seated so close I can see the guinea pig's dark red eyes, which look like beads of blood.

"My aim with little Chimera," Pop says, petting the animal's white fur and pink petal ears, "is to challenge what we define as genetically pure. What we define as otherness."

The guinea pig squirms in Pop's arms, squeaking like a baby's squeeze toy.

"Green fluorescent protein," Pop says, "doesn't change the creature in any significant way but one."

Just then, angry shouts erupt in the lobby.

Pop's booming voice says, "But what tremendous importance we place on that one thing."

The theatre's back doors bang open, and we all swivel in our seats. The picketers march through, chanting, "Hell, no, we won't glow!" One protestor tosses leaflets in the air. A woman in an aisle seat jumps up and tries to wrestle away a placard, but she stumbles backward with a yelp into some guy's lap. Meanwhile, the beefy doorman storms in, red-faced and growling, "*Câlisse de tabarnak!*"

Ruby-Doo turns toward me, his left leg brushing against my right . . . and I swear I want to move away, but my leg stays put.

"Bedlam," he says with a grin.

"Totally," I whisper.

Up onstage, Pop nods toward the projection room. Off go all the house lights. For two seconds, pitch blackness. Then a loud click. Then a bluish shaft of light beaming down from the rafters.

In Pop's arms, the white guinea pig turns a brilliant green. Like crème de menthe. Like a traffic light telling you to go. Like the glowing skin of Frankenstein's monster.

It's very weird and really scary.

And kind of beautiful in an unexpected way.

THE B9ERS

JOHN SMITH LIES on his doctor's exam table with his trousers bunched at his ankles and his derriere stuck to the table's paper runner. His testicles are swollen and bruised purple: two overripe plums. Up one side of his scrotum is a puckered inch-long scar threaded with black stitching.

Dr. Libman pokes a gloved finger where the blood has pooled in John's groin. "How does this feel, John?"

Wincing, John says, "Gosh, doc, still a bit tender."

A week ago, Dr. Libman snipped out a lump of tissue that had clung to John's left testicle like a burr. ("Benign tumour," the doctor had said. "Sounds almost oxymoronic, doesn't it?") After the surgery, John expected to be a spanking new man. Instead, he's felt mildly depressed all week, as if his new lease on life is for an apartment with clanging radiators and leaky faucets.

"What's still got me baffled, doc," John says from the exam table as he tugs up his trousers, "is how the darned thing grew there in the first place." John jogs daily. Shies away from red meat, shuns dairy. No cigarettes, no illicit drugs. For Pete's sake, he treats his body like a temple, and what happens? A depraved sect moves in and starts worshipping.

Dr. Libman peels off his latex gloves with a thwack. He's got big fleshy paws, hands John can't imagine doing the dainty lady's work of sewing up scrotums. The doctor sinks into a swivel chair and laces his sausage fingers together as if to play Here's the Church, Here's the Steeple. The steeple he points at John. "We can't claim responsibility," he says, "for all our body's aberrations."

Later that afternoon, the body's aberrations haunt John as he works at Clean, his soap shop. John is dressing the shop's front window with a female mannequin in a hooded raincoat and rubber boots. The mannequin wields a Super Soaker water gun filled with Bakteria Buster, a powerful antibacterial soap invented by his grandmother, Grandma Lu, who died when he was just a young lad.

When he finishes in the window, he closes the shop and goes up to his loft above Clean. He hasn't got around to replacing his furniture, which Nuko, his ex-girlfriend, absconded with when she moved out six months ago. The thick beige carpeting is still patterned with geometric depressions where the furniture once stood. The effect is of those crop figures extraterrestrials cut into fields of wheat.

That evening, when his bruise starts to throb and his stitches start to itch, John inches down into a tubful of Mighty Mousse bubble bath. As he relaxes in the steaming foam, he wonders whether he should have phoned Nuko about his tumour. She'd left John for a cobbler, whom she moved in with immediately. With a doleful look, she informed John that cobbling was a dying art. The poor cobbler was broke; hence she needed the furniture. John recalls what Nuko said as the moving van carted his stuff off to the cobbler's.

"God, John, why are you so frigging nice?"

A few days after John's appointment with Dr. Libman, he cycles over to the hospital and thumbtacks a homemade poster to the bulletin board in the Oncology waiting room.

THE B9ERS.

SUPPORT FOR VICTIMS OF

BENIGN TUMOURS.

HOW HARMLESS IS BENIGN?

At the bottom of the poster are his name and number. His idea: to start a group where members can swap stories and maybe come to understand their bodies' duplicity. Two days later, while he's at the back sink scrubbing the scalp of a homeless man who stops by Clean weekly for a free shampoo, the phone rings. It's a woman calling about the B9ers. Her name is Tutsi.

"Like Tootsie Roll?" asks John.

"No, like the Bantu people killed in Rwanda," says Tutsi. "I changed my name to help keep their memory alive. It's not much, but sometimes a lot of little efforts make a world of difference."

They meet that evening on the stairs of the history museum. Tutsi is a freckly young woman in low-slung bell-bottoms. Her auburn dreadlocks are tied atop her head like a bonsai tree. Her eyes are a tarsier's: big, inquisitive, set close together. John is a little bit in love already, but, frankly, what woman is he not secretly a bit in love with? His shop clerk with her sexy bleached moustache, his female customers, even his late Grandma Lu (her picture on the Bakteria Buster bottle—steely-eyed and buxom—he finds strangely arousing).

John has brought along a tape recorder. Tutsi has brought along a big Tupperware container. She peels off the lid to reveal two dozen muffins, still warm. "Oat bran and banana," she says. "I hand them out to the sex workers along Theodore Avenue. Gets a little fibre into them."

She passes John a muffin. He nibbles at the hot little bundle. "Mmmm," he says. They get down to the interview, the tape recorder and muffins between them on the stairs. "Our tumours are called benign," John begins. "But I see them as a wakeup call."

"Or an alarm clock going off accidentally at four in the morning," says Tutsi. She explains that, despite her strict macrobiotic diet, a tumour bloomed in her colon.

"Mine was in my groin area," John says shyly, and his testicle throbs like a rubber bicycle horn squeezed.

"I'm the type of gal who looks for a silver lining," says Tutsi brightly.

"What's the silver lining with your tumour?"

"Maybe the smiley face," Tutsi says. She pulls up her T-shirt a little to uncover her scar: a red crescent two inches long below her navel. "You see the face?" she asks, and John does see it. Two black moles on her stomach for the eyes, her outtie belly button for a pug nose, the crescent scar for an upturned mouth. A smiley face looking back at him.

"Holy mackerel!"

They talk for an hour. About the discovery of their lumps. About that disoriented feeling they now have, which Tutsi likens to the headlong rush of stepping off a moving sidewalk at the airport. At one point, John brings up his Grandma Lu, her motives for making soap: "She'd say, 'Strip naked a banker and a hobo, and the only difference, by God, is the ripeness of their B.O.'" With his support group, John's mission is to strip the members down, figuratively speaking, to learn how they differ from your average Joe Blow. That difference, he speculates, is key to understanding their tumours.

At ten o'clock, Tutsi has to leave for her muffin route, and she invites John along. All goes fine till one prostitute, a transsexual walking like a palsied pigeon, grabs the open Tupperware bowl and chucks it into the street.

John chases the runaway muffins as they roll toward a sewer grate.

"That happens sometimes," Tutsi explains afterwards, the metal stud in her tongue clicking against her teeth.

"You don't get discouraged?" John asks.

Tutsi's reply: "There but for the grace of my own personal Higher Power go I."

The next day at Clean, John picks up the phone to call the supplier of Scottie's Scouring Scrub, but before he can dial, a cheery voice exclaims, "Greetings and salutations!"

His name is Manny. He's a B9er.

John meets this fellow on Saturday afternoon at the corner of Berry and Caple. "I'll be the one with the three-legged dog," Manny says on the phone, and sure enough a basset hound with a missing hind leg is with him. Baggy eyes, jowls, drool and dander—that's the dog. Tubby, bald, spectacles the size of quarters, a grinning face like a snowman's—that's Manny. In his hands is a jar that once held jumbo pickles. "I brought this baby along," Manny says, jiggling the jar. Inside, floating in a formaldehyde broth, is the man's extracted stomach tumour. The thing resembles a discarded muddy softball chewed apart by his dog.

"Thought we'd have us a little show and tell," Manny says with a wink. "Ain't she a beaut?"

John turns on his tape recorder and attaches it to his belt. They walk down the street, John in a linen suit and silk tie, Manny in his Hawaiian shirt and Bermuda shorts. It's a sunny day. The double-headed parking meters cast Mickey Mouse ears onto the sidewalk.

"Take your time, Spigot!" Manny says to the dog hopping along behind. They hurry across the street to a neighbourhood park with regal maple trees and peony plants with pink flowers so top-heavy they're kowtowing. The city plans to turn this park into housing, and some local residents are gathering today to halt the project. Manny explained all this during his phone call to John. "There's a tie-in with our tumours," Manny promised, and John wonders what the dickens that connection might be.

The residents have congregated at the park's far end, fifty people of all ages and lots of leaping dogs, their leashes entwining in a game of cat's cradle. Manny points out the city councillor, a man with a hedgehog hairpiece who's waving his arms as he warns about dirty syringes left in the park by drug addicts. "Thirty-three so far this year!" he bellows. "Syringes your children might jab innocently into a vein!"

When the city councillor wraps up his spiel, Manny climbs up on a park bench. "Guess what I do for a living, folks?" he asks the crowd, who squint up at him. "Tree surgeon—I cut disease out of poplars and willows and beech and cedars and all our tall, leafy friends."

How ironic! John thinks. Manny up in a tree with his dog is what he's imagining. Manny requesting a scalpel and Spigot slapping it into his palm.

"These babies," Manny says, "these Norwegian maples here, that grove of skyrocket junipers there, they're all vulnerable to disease." The crowd swivel their heads around to take in the trees. "Trees are our city's lungs. They breathe out oxygen to purify the atmosphere. But they also filter the smog and guck clogging our air. So it's no wonder they sometimes get sick."

Manny grins broadly as he holds up his pickle jar. "This here is a tumour. Was it cut out of a maple or a fir? Neither, ladies and gents, it was cut out of me."

A few gasps here.

What guts, John thinks.

"Mr. City Councillor," Manny implores, "cut down all these trees, our city's air filters, and you'll get more people like me with hunks of diseased tissue to be sliced out of their bellies."

Later, after the crowd has applauded and the city councillor has made a lukewarm promise to rethink his support for the housing project, Manny walks John to his bus stop. Along the way, Manny talks about the deathwatch beetle, a hairy insect with a mouth like garden shears that has infested the maple trees in the park.

"It's a very picky eater," Manny explains. "It lives strictly off the bark of the Norwegian maple."

That evening, in his bathtub, John muses that maybe the B9ers are like the Norwegian maple. If he could only figure out what their hairy deathwatch beetle is. The wax on bell peppers? The arsenic in pressed wood? The oat bran in muffins? Maybe the glue fumes rising from wall-to-wall carpeting?

A few days later, John is still chewing this matter over as he sits in a stranger's living room. Beside him are floor-to-ceiling shelves crammed with books, stubby candles, dusty birthday cards, chipped knickknacks.

"Talking with people in the same boat might help us," John calls out.

In the kitchen just off the living room, a woman says, "Help us with closure—isn't that the word everybody tosses around?" After pouring two glasses of grapefruit juice, she adds, "Though maybe we only really get closure when our coffin lids slam shut." The woman, who's in her early fifties, enunciates like a speech therapist. She carries the glasses into the living room and sets them down on the coffee table. She's tall and wiry with pale skin and a grey ponytail. She wears knee-length khaki shorts and walking shoes with thick soles. On the coffee table atop John's tape recorder is her business card: SUNNY ATKINS, UNCLUTTERER.

Sunny sits in an armchair across from John. "I apologize for the mess," she says, even though this townhouse belongs not to her but to her client, a history professor away for the week. John asks what an unclutterer does, and Sunny explains that she simplifies people's lives by rearranging their kitchen cabinets, downsizing their wardrobes, wading through all the flotsam and jetsam they accumulate. People have fifteen tea towels, thirty sweaters, six shampoos, Sunny says. She teaches them to make do with less.

"My husband jokes I'd get rid of my second kidney if I could. *Two! Who needs two?*" Sunny sips her juice. "When that lump showed up in my breast, I thought I'd be making do with one. I was petrified. But then the lump was benign and Dr. Libman removed it, and now I'm supposed to resume my life. But I keep thinking, What else is floating around in there?" Sunny taps a finger against her abdomen. "How many other clumps of cells still too small to detect are madly multiplying?"

John smiles sympathetically. Sunny smiles back. "Dr. Libman points out that I'm one of the lucky women." Touching a hand to her breast, she adds, "So why do I feel I've won the booby prize?"

———

One early evening a week later, John is at home, lying on the carpet in his housecoat. Beside him, atop a Japanese sushi table, is his tape recorder. He's been listening to his interviews with the B9ers. Also on the table are library books about tumours, books so maddeningly arcane that whenever he skims the pages, a nestful of questions squawk up at him like baby birds.

It's time for him to call the B9ers to set up their first meeting. Oh, if only he had some answers! Doesn't he owe it to these people? What a nice bunch, too. Not a whiner or self-pitier among them. In fact, if he had to name a common denominator, it would be this: the B9ers are darn nice.

Presently he dozes off. Who knows how long he's asleep before his door buzzer buzzes. He staggers up and pushes the intercom button.

"Excuse me for bothering you, sir," a voice says. "My name is Lawrence Arnold, and I represent the McFarland Boarding School for Orphaned Boys. Could I take a few minutes of your time?"

"Sure, sure," John says. He opens the door. Up the stairs comes a slender young fellow in his early twenties. A crew cut. A white wrinkled dress shirt and navy blue tie. A worn briefcase. He shakes John's hand.

"Come in, come in," John says, and they end up sitting on the floor, the sushi table between them.

"The McFarland School," Lawrence Arnold begins, "was founded in 1922 by Cecil McFarland, a former mayor of our proud city who himself—this is a true fact—was an orphan. Now, Mr. McFarland didn't believe a boy's financial status should prevent him from getting the best education. He saw education as a stepping stone toward a brilliant future. Wouldn't you agree, sir?"

John stares at the young man's face: a widow's peak, eyes the colour of a blue jay. "Sorry, I'm in a bit of a daze," John finally mumbles. "I was just taking a short nap."

"Well, let me apologize for waking you, sir," says Lawrence Arnold. "Winston Churchill was a power napper himself. Feeds the intellect." The young man taps a finger against his temple. "I learned that at the school. Yes, I'm a McFarland graduate." He unzips his briefcase and takes out a brochure, which he spreads across the books on the sushi table. "This here's the school. It's out in the country near Tuckerville, so there's fewer distractions and the boys can knuckle down."

John looks at the brochure. The school is Gothic. A vine-covered bell tower. Lawrence Arnold is now gabbing on about government cutbacks and the need to invest in our nation's youth. He mentions a dona- tion: "Something in the twenty-dollar range." John gets up and goes to the kitchen, where his wallet lies atop the bread box. What a sweet kid, John thinks. Though maybe one day that sweet, innocent kid with two first names will wake up with a lump in his stom- ach or his intestines or his scrotum.

"You just moving in?" Lawrence Arnold says con- versationally from the other side of the loft.

"Redecorating" is John's excuse for his sparse fur- nishings. He goes to pluck a twenty from his wallet, but out comes a blank cheque. He ends up writing "one hundred" on the amount line.

"Who do I make this out to?" John asks, waving the cheque.

"Actually, sir, we prefer cash," Lawrence Arnold says.

In John's eyes, the entire loft tilts slightly and then rights itself.

The next evening at Clean, Spigot lifts his head, squeezes his bloodshot eyes shut and emits a jaw- distorting yawn. The dog is lying beneath a table dis- playing bars of glycerine soap stacked in a pyramid. Now and then, his tail thumps against the floor.

The B9ers have gathered for their first official meeting. Tutsi, Manny and Sunny are seated in a half circle. A fourth unoccupied chair is John's, but he's too nervous to sit, and so he stands near the shampoo sink. They've all come, he thinks, grateful and a little surprised. Last night, when he conjectured over the phone to them about why their tumours had taken root, they could have laughed at him, but none of them did. They listened. They asked questions. They agreed to put John's idea to the test.

Near the checkout counter, on an upside-down wooden soapbox, stands Lawrence Arnold. John invited him with a promise of additional donations to the school for orphans.

"One recent McFarland graduate," Lawrence Arnold says near the end of his speech, "launched a computer start-up that's pulled in a million bucks." Is it John's imagination or is the young man tenser than last night? He keeps fingering his tie. Lifting his arm a moment ago, he flashed a damp half-moon stain in his armpit.

Tutsi raises her hand to speak. John is expecting this. "To give him a chance," she said to John on the phone. To Lawrence Arnold, she says, "We B9ers are a support group. As you know, we're all recovering from having a lump of flesh cut out of our bodies. We're all very vulnerable people, Lawrence Arnold. Can you understand that vulnerability?"

"Hey, maybe a McFarland boy will one day find a cure for tumours," Lawrence Arnold proposes. "I mean, for the real ones, the cancerous ones. Wouldn't that be great?"

Tutsi turns and mouths "Okay" to John. Sunny and Manny also glance over at John. For the first time since John's operation, his scrotum doesn't itch. He thinks of Nuko. A pity she isn't here to see him now.

From his pants pocket, John pulls out a purple pistol.

He aims that pistol. He fires.

An amber stream of Bakteria Buster shoots across the room and soaks Lawrence Arnold's left ear.

"What the . . . !" the young man cries, his hand flying up to his head.

Manny, Tutsi and Sunny have pulled their own purple pistols from handbags and backpacks. Three squirts fly. Lawrence Arnold's white shirt is now streaked with Bakteria Buster. He stumbles off the soapbox.

"You crazy motherfuckers!" Lawrence Arnold hollers, backing in behind the checkout counter.

Manny shouts, "Fire!"

And the B9ers do.

"Jesus H. Christ!" Lawrence Arnold screams. He throws his hands up like a movie star hounded by paparazzi. Bakteria Buster splatters across his clothes.

John throws down his pistol, dashes to the window display and, from the arms of the mannequin, plucks the Super Soaker water gun. He aims, pulls the trigger. A whoosh of water splashes Lawrence Arnold in the face. The young man falls to his knees, crying "My eyes! My eyes!" but he's faking, John knows, because Bakteria Buster is guaranteed tear-free.

"You should be ashamed," Sunny scolds. "Taking advantage of orphans."

Lawrence Arnold is now rolling on the floor. He slaps the linoleum and stomps his feet.

The B9ers gather around him.

"Oh, my!" says Tutsi.

"Don't worry, son," Manny says, "soap washes out."

John sets down the Super Soaker and goes to the sink to wet a facecloth under the tap. He bends down beside Lawrence Arnold and wipes the young man's face. "There, there," he says. Lawrence Arnold sits up, dazed, a dust bunny clinging to the back of his head. "I got to go home now," he says, suddenly calm. John puts his arm around Lawrence Arnold and pulls him to his feet while the others hold their pistols to their sides, sheepish bank robbers in a bungled heist.

"I got to go home," Lawrence Arnold repeats.

"Let me explain," John says, holding the young man's wet sleeve, but Lawrence Arnold pulls away, grabs his briefcase and bolts out the front door, the store bell ringing behind him.

"We should go after him," Manny says, but no one moves.

Finally, Sunny sits down hard in her chair. "Well, if you can't beat 'em," she says, "beat 'em up."

"I feel malignant," Tutsi says. Her dreadlocks hang like droopy bulrushes.

John reminds the B9ers that you've got to use a little soap to wash away soap scum. He looks at the dejected group. Last night on the phone, they each listened so patiently as he explained his theory: that when you're as benign as a dodo bird, what prevents the enemy from sailing a boat to your shore and clubbing you over the head? Were they fiercer, more ruthless, John was suggesting, maybe their tumours wouldn't have sprouted. Last night, John was convinced that the very benignity of the B9ers was their hairy deathwatch beetle. But now, as he looks down at the damp balled-up facecloth in his hand, he's not so certain.

"You sure that guy's a con artist?" Tutsi asks.

"No ifs, ands or buts," John says. To double-check, though, he had called the McFarland School this morning. Yes, a student by the name of Lawrence Arnold had attended the institution a few years back. "A big, bright boy," the secretary on the phone reminisced. "He won full scholarship to the Poppleton College for People of Colour."

Though John tells them not to bother, the B9ers help him clean up. Tutsi mops. Sunny wipes the counters. Manny quietens down Spigot, who has erupted into a barking fit. "Shh, shh," Manny whispers, stroking the dog's back. "It's okay. That's my boy."

As if the words are directed at him, John starts to calm down. He takes a few deep breaths. He collects the water pistols and throws them in the trash. He avoids looking at the other B9ers. Finally, they leave, each one scurrying off in a different direction, each one mumbling that John should keep in touch.

He won't, though. He never wants to see them again.

A half-hour later, while ordering a BLT hold the B at the sandwich place next door, John discovers his wallet missing from his back pocket.

———

Before any other B9er can call, John cycles to the hospital and pulls down his poster. His guilt is a burnt pancake on a griddle that he has to scrape off with Scottie's Scouring Scrub. He wonders whether he strong-armed the group into the attack on the phony Lawrence Arnold. To persuade the B9ers, didn't he play up the poor-orphan angle? The exploitation, the ignominy?

His stolen wallet he considers a light sentence, all things considered. He recalls Lawrence Arnold's fit and, though it's so out of character for him, he occasionally has the same urge to throw himself on the ground for a tantrum. Like three weeks after the B9ers' meeting when, at the post office, he spots Nuko ahead of him in line, the cobbler's arm around her waist. But his anger soon wanes and he feels chagrined. Not because he pictures Nuko and the cobbler reclining on his sofa or because he feels he's been too gullible, but because he sees the guile and pettiness in them and, even more distressing, sees the guile and pettiness in himself.

On the way home from the post office, he goes into a furniture store and orders himself a new sofa.

Weeks later, during a late summer afternoon, John stumbles across a newspaper article, "Unclutter Your

Life," written by Sunny Atkins. The article is about how cleaning out your shoe closet can banish negativity from your world.

As John skims the article, a white woman in a sari and flip-flops comes up to the checkout counter to moan about the unusually hot summer. "Those damn SUVs are triggering a global warming," she complains. So incensed is she that John almost passes her Sunny's article. Another customer, a fellow in a blue baseball cap, brings his purchase to the counter. As John rings up the man's bottle of soap, the woman in the sari gripes to them both, "SUV should really stand for Slaughter Us Vehicles."

She's still prattling on a minute later when John notices that the customer in the baseball cap has left his wallet on the counter. John grabs it and hurries out of the cool store and into the street. Outside, the air feels as warm and thick as porridge. A few blocks north, John thinks he sees a blue baseball cap. He trots after his customer, even though no one is minding Clean. By the time he's run five blocks, his shirt is sticking to the small of his back. He stops. A woman comes out of a shoe store in a blast of air conditioning. John glances around, but he's lost the blue cap.

He turns and heads back to Clean. Down a side street, though, he spots the man in the baseball cap waiting at a bus stop.

"Excuse me!"

The man slowly turns.

"You forgot something," John calls out as he jogs over.

John holds out the wallet, but the man doesn't take it. He's wearing the aviator sunglasses he kept on in Clean. He reaches up and removes his glasses. He yanks off his cap.

He has a widow's peak and blue eyes.

"Hey!" John says. He glances down at the black leather wallet he's holding.

His old wallet.

"Jeez!"

A grin from Lawrence Arnold's impostor. "How are the B9ers, sir?" he says.

"We disbanded," John blurts out. "Jeez!" he repeats.

"So sorry to hear that, sir," the young man replies. Then: "I'm in detox now. Went in shortly after my soaping." He lifts up his shopping bag from Clean, shakes it. Inside is a bottle of Bakteria Buster.

"You mean we helped you?" John says, astounded. Is this another con job?

The bus pulls up.

"Folks like you," the young man says, "you can't help helping. It's in your nature."

He steps onto the bus.

As the bus pulls away, the young man waves.

John waves back. He keeps waving till the bus is out of sight. Then he flips open his wallet: his cards are there, so is sixty bucks. He pockets the wallet and starts back to Clean.

Gosh, how peculiar, he thinks. How very odd!

On the way, John passes a Scotch pine rising from the sidewalk. Its blue-green needles have a silvery tinge. A lump the size of John's hand is growing just above where the first branch juts out. John reaches up and strokes that lump. He feels the city's toxicity being neutralized beneath the bark.

BANG CRUNCH

YOU ARE EEPIE CARPETROD. You're eight years old and attend Albert Einstein Elementary, and you're a perfectly normal girl, at least till that day in Mrs. Mendelwort's class when you draw a multi-coloured crayon creature that has a yellow face with buggy eyes and a pug nose, a hat sprouting a garden-hose valve, an armless blue rectangle of a chest, thimbles for breasts, shapely red legs bent at the knees, and feet jammed into high heels. Very Joan Miró, Mrs. Mendelwort says. Her knowledge of surrealism is bang on but her pronunciation is off and so you correct her, *zho-an mee-ro,* you say, and you tell her that Miró preferred the Catalan pronunciation and then glance down at your reproduction of Miró's *Fleeing Young Girl* and up at your teacher, whose mouth mirrors your creature's mouth, crumpled surprise. After school you walk home to your apartment building, where out front, skating down the handicapped ramp, is the super's son, a curly-haired teenager with a clipped bark like a Jack Russell terrier's, and Roy barks and you say, Gilles de la Tourette's syndrome? His rain-puddle look confirms your suspicion. The rusty elevator screeches you up to your apartment, where your single mum, hands sheathed in oven mitts, is coaxing a squirrel out from where it's wedged between the screen and the window-pane, while over on the coffee table sit the innards of the television because your mum has been dusting the tubes again. Have you taken your meds? you ask, and you point out that Divalproex is effective against both rapid-cycling and non-rapid-cycling episodes. As the squirrel chatters hysterically, you think, I must be gifted, but this gift is as welcome as day-of-the-week underwear at Christmas. Your mum, bewildered by your ballooning vocabulary, takes you to the doctor's for a three-month-long battery of tests, and in between these tests you master longhand and long division, read *Madame Bovary,* grow twelve inches, and when all the results are back your mum breaks down and curses herself for calling you Eepie, an old lady's name, because the doctor has just explained that you have Fred Hoyle syndrome, a rare disease that, although it boosts your brainpower exponentially, has begun aging you a month a day so that on the way home you need to stop at the drugstore for panty shields and antiperspirant. Later, while she calls your relatives and weeps, you hear barking and slide open your bedroom window and in the alleyway below see Roy clambering out of a Dumpster, a bent hula hoop in hand. Roy is sixteen. You are sixteen. Yet *your* sixteen has been stuffed into eight years and eight months. When you've climbed down the fire escape, Roy asks, New in town? because with breasts and your mum's miniskirt you're no longer recognizable. The vein in his biceps, you tell him, reminds you of the rubber tube the blood-test nurse at the hospital tied around your arm, and then you talk about syndromes as he leads you to the basement of your apartment building, to a big storage locker wrapped in chicken wire, where he sculpts found objects into art, his latest work a nest of coat hangers from which emerges an umbrella stripped bare, skeletal fingers thrown up jubilantly. Jubilant, you say, and he lifts your head and plants his lips on your forehead and minutes go by and he doesn't kiss you and then he does. You make love on a beanbag chair the colour of macaroni and cheese and when Roy enters you, you nuzzle his neck and inhale his smell of vegetable peelings from the Dumpster, and your orgasm feels like a hundred glimmering goldfish expelled through the hole in an aquarium. You realize that if you love this boy, your love, under the circumstances, will have to be fleeting. You don't tell your mum about Roy. As usual, she brings you to the Joy Wah, a Chinese restaurant where you chopstick broccoli and bean curd into your mouth while on the karaoke stage your mum sings in dulcet tones that you light up her life, give her hope to carry on, and when you were eight you hung on every word and lionized your mum but now you think about quantum physics, about the intrinsic differences between Sunni and Shiite, about the blue vein in Roy's biceps and its smaller counterpart piping through his penis. Soon school ends. In the past months you've skipped grades eight times and coincidentally in every grade a big-boned girl briefly befriended you only to mock you later, saying for example that your hair, once honey blond, had gone mousey with age. In the summertime your mum quits her job as postmistress and becomes your impresario, passing you off as a genius diviner to the neighbours, who line up at your bedroom door for a consultation. Ask her anything, your mum says. Also: No personal cheques. What they ask about is themselves, like will they ever lose weight, take a lover, find happiness, buy a BMW, confront their fathers, win the snooker playoff, and these are questions you can't answer but you feign clairvoyance, tilting your head pensively. Roy lines up at your door, shrugging his shoulders in a Tourette's tic, and your mum says, Who knows how that guy pays, and you know because you give him part of your cut. Roy always has an interesting question, such as why do hooded seals inflate a red balloon out their nose during courtship, and you answer and think, How sad that he never asks anything about himself, such as will he outgrow the shrugging and barking. Soon your mum wrangles you an advice column, "Ask Eepie," in the local newspaper, which you like because you sometimes invent letters about, say, the role of halocarbons in the greenhouse effect. On your ninth birthday, you turn thirty-six and your column turns into a cable talk show and Mrs. Mendelwort, your third-grade teacher, is booked as your first guest and she brings along the fleeing young girl, your old drawing, which she presents to you, pronouncing *Joan* the Catalan way, but soon she starts crying because her husband, she's ashamed to say, is a gasoline sniffer. You try to comfort your guests but your suggestions to them are more albino pigeons than doves of peace. Your advice usually boils down to: Act quickly, act graciously. After your guests blow their noses into the hankies that your mum embroiders with the show's name, *Through the Ages,* they usually apologize for their tears and the blue lady, her skin a denim colour from ingesting colloidal silver, wonders how she can cry when you, Eepie Carpetrod, won't live much beyond your tenth birthday. Your mum argues you're eternal, that your mind and soul will expand forever like the universe, an allusion to the Big Bang theory, which you explained to her over lunch, tomato soup and saltines, but you know what your death will be, your brain collapsing under its own weight, the Big Crunch. In the chicken-wire workshop, you and Roy talk matter-of-factly about life and death, Roy theorizing that you are the future of mankind because man's life is too long, it's killing the planet, and he picks up your empty tomato soup can and says that if we lived only a decade think how many fewer soup cans we'd litter the countryside with. How do you feel about your impending death? You're not sure. Ever since you began to speed-age, your range of emotions has narrowed into the yellow line on a highway crossing the Prairies. That constant, that middle-of-the-road. Roy unrolls a sheet of bubble wrap, saying that each bubble represents a story in our lives and when each story ends we pop a bubble and when no more bubbles are left it's time to fertilize the grass. With your thumb you crush a bubble and the pop coincides with his bark and you both laugh, then you straddle Roy on the beanbag and when you're coming you open your eyes to a blinding flash. An orgasmic illusion? No—a man in a beanie snapping your picture from outside the chicken wire. Naked, Roy chases Beanie, yelling Fuck off!, and he must be furious because he never swears for fear his cursing will be taken as a progression of his Tourette's. Your picture makes the pages of a tabloid, a fetching photo what with the blush in your cheeks and your hand entwined in Roy's hair, his curls five rings around your fingers. The shameless lust of Eepie Carpetrod, your mum reads to you. Please no finger wagging, you tell her and your mum says, Who's wagging? Also: This could be good for ratings. She's right. Your ratings rocket up but your guests are now petulant, like the housewife with Munchausen's syndrome, who, when you scold her for sprinkling arsenic into her water glass, calls you a hussy. The police come sniffing, but who to arrest?— a forty-seven-year-old woman loving a sixteen-year-old boy or a sixteen-year-old boy loving a nine-year-old girl?—and in the end no one's charged although *Through the Ages* is cancelled owing to a brawl in the studio audience that leaves a pregnant woman with a stab wound in her belly from a freshly sharpened HP pencil and when she miscarries people scream Baby Killer! at you even though your cameraman wielded the pencil. Your fame morphs first into notoriety then, poof, into has-beenism. Your mum, under the mistaken impression you need cheering up, invites Roy to move in and so you and his super father, a kind man with pointy, widely spaced teeth like an alligator clip, help Roy lug his found objects into the spare room, his new workshop. Your mum and Roy get along like two scoops of ice cream seeing as they both love to twist apart toasters and telephones and cobble them back together and they eventually gut your computer, Roy Jack-Russelling and your mum singing about that night the lights went out in Georgia. Roy turns seventeen. You turn sixty-two. You have a skunky streak of grey in your hair but your skin is still unwrinkled, your cumulative exposure to sunlight being only nine and a half years. Your mum suggests a project, an autobiography, for which she presents you with a leather-bound journal, Barbie's face pasted on the front, Einstein's face pasted on the back. You will translate your life into a story, obviously a short one.

You start in third person but your mum says, Too impersonal, and so you try first person but the "I" looks flimsy, as hopeless as a lone chopstick, and then Roy inspires you to use "you" because he's talking to you about you and keeps saying you, that in your story you should write what you taste like and smell like, that you taste like orange zest and you smell like rubber worms in a box of fishing tackle. One day, walking along a highway on the lookout for found objects not yet found, you explain to Roy the Big Rip theory, whereby the universe's dark energy will eventually tear the cosmos apart, and just then a guy in a speeding pickup tosses a cardboard box out his window and the box rips apart littering the road with a litter of kittens. Cursing the universe's dark energy, Roy frees the sole survivor from a clump of cushioning weeds and then cradles the mewling tabby and suggests naming her after that Egyptian goddess with the cat's head, What's her name again? You snap around for the answer and finally say, Bastet, while Roy stares at you, shocked by your hesitation. He sets the kitten down and encircles you in his arms. It's started, you say. He kisses your brow, temples and earlobes as you close your eyes and listen to the whimpers of the kitten you'll name not Bastet but Gnab, *bang* spelled backwards. At night in bed, Gnab asleep between you, Roy whispers that maybe you'll contract back to age eight and then burst back to age seventy-eight, up and down, forever and ever, and you trace a finger up and down the hillocks of his spine and say, You never know, and he muffles a sob into his pillow because you *always* know. The contraction is much faster than the expansion. You de-age a year a day. Roy continually trims your ponytail and within two weeks the silver in your hair disappears and your mum lifts a lock suspiciously and you lie, Nice and Easy Ash Blond, since the truth will knock her off her meds. Roy disagrees about telling your mum and the two of you argue over this at a table at the Joy Wah while onstage your mum sings about baby crying the day the circus came to town. At first, hiding the truth is easy. When your mum asks about the missing tampons you lie that Roy is using them for a sculpture but by age twenty your face takes on its old baby-fat look, cheeks like scones, and then one morning your forehead sprouts a pimple as conspicuous as a nipple and your mum twigs to the truth and handcuffs her fingers around your wrists and murmurs, How long? You look her in the eye. Two and a half weeks, you say. She grasps your head in her hands as if through your skull she feels your brain shrivelling. Roy comes out of his workshop. I'm finished, he says. He leads you into the shop, where a velvet curtain is draped over his latest sculpture. It stands as tall as Roy. Roy grips the corner of the curtain and pulls. You hear two synchronized intakes of breath. Yours and your mum's. A sunny yellow face, a red hat with a valve, an armless blue box for a chest, red mannequin legs in flight. The fleeing young girl is now three-dimensional. In front of this girl, you and your mum sink to your knees. Your mum is crying. And you, incredibly, are also crying. Roy, his shoulders jumping in a non-stop shrug, folds the velvet curtain as Gnab bats at its tasselled trim. Roy's gift is the most beautiful you've ever received. You know what you'll do with this girl. You must write this idea down soon, these last wishes of yours, because in no time at all you'll be six years old and illiterate and then a toddler in a crib and then an embryo in a receiving blanket and then an ovum and a spermatozoa drifting apart. Roy kneels beside you and your mum. All three of you hold hands. You in the middle. You squeeze their hands, spelling out *thanks* in Morse code. You gaze at the fleeing girl and imagine her in your graveyard, a vivid apparition surrounded by a field of drab grey rectangles. A colourful tombstone commemorating your full life. Joan Miró, you decide, was wrong. The girl isn't fleeing. She's not running away, she's running in place. Very fast.

SCRAPBOOK

A DIAGRAM OF A BUILDING

Robertson Hall has lost its roof. It's as if a twister has blown the top off the building to reveal the mouse maze of classrooms and corridors on its fifth floor.

The diagram appears in *Maclean's* magazine. Amy wonders who drew it. A man, she assumes. A man with the clinical fortitude of a coroner. He's peopled his diagram with stick figures. They walk the hallways, bend over drinking fountains, raise their hands in class. Perhaps they're thinking what a fine institution Scott University is. And Petertown, what a peaceful community.

The stick figures, Amy notes, are shadowy grey. Except in room 523. The eight women huddled together on one side of the German class are pale pink. The five men lined up on the other side are deep purple. Like good boys, these purple men filed out of the room when Buddy MacDonald told them to.

Where's Buddy? The question is like Where's Waldo? But Amy doesn't need to search long. She knows where Buddy is: the women's washroom down the hall from the German class. Buddy is the red stick figure. He's lying in a toilet stall, a chunk of his head floating in the toilet bowl. Brain, scalp, skin, skull. Buddy got down on his knees, leaned over that bowl. In one hand he held a gun, a silencer attached to its barrel. He put the gun to his temple and squeezed the trigger.

THE LABEL FROM A PRESCRIPTION BOTTLE

"In the pink" is the expression her parents use for sound health. Amy has always been in the pink. If she has taken prescription medication in her twenty-three years, she doesn't remember. Consequently, although the pills are intended for her boyfriend, Thomas, her name typed on the label seems portentous.

This afternoon, she went to the campus clinic and feigned insomnia. She could have told the truth: her boyfriend had been in room 523. But she lied. "I knew one of the girls who were killed," she told the doctor, who then scribbled on a prescription pad.

The prescription was for sleeping pills, and she's now sitting at the kitchen table, crushing a tablet with the back of a spoon. She mixes the powder with some applesauce because Thomas has trouble swallowing pills whole.

Thomas's face is flushed with blood. He's in the living room, doing the downward dog on a yoga mat, his hands and feet flat on the floor, his rear end pointing up, his head dangling between his extended arms. He looks like no dog Amy has ever seen, certainly not like Bugaboo, their female Dalmatian.

His German parents nicknamed Thomas *der Gepard*—the cheetah—a tribute to his gracefulness and speed. But despite his streamlined body, wide-set hazel eyes, and mane of tawny dreadlocks, Amy doesn't see a big cat either. She sees simply a man. A man down on all fours. She recalls the first time she lay naked in bed with Thomas, how she inspected the meat of his calves, his flat, bluish nipples, the walnut folds of his testicles. She thought, So this is a man.

Thomas puffs out a last gusty exhale as the brooks on their relaxation tape stop babbling. "How many pills did you mix in?" he asks when Amy brings over his mug of applesauce.

"Just one."

"I need two."

"The label says one tablet at bedtime. You've never taken these before. You could have an allergic reaction or be extra sensitive."

"Spare me the lecture, Amy." He rubs his eyes. "I haven't slept in days. Just give me another fucking pill."

Later, as they lie in bed, Amy wonders whether in the night Thomas will again whisper, "Do you still love me?" Will he curl himself around her again? God, she hopes not. She can't stand his touch. Yet she can't bear to push him away.

She turns to him now. He has dozed off. He's so quiet and still that she's struck with the irrational fear that two pills might constitute an overdose. She holds her breath. When he makes a soft smacking sound with his lips, she breathes out. She whispers, "Yes, I do." She says it not to him but to herself and to her witnesses: the spill of moonlight across the ceiling, the glowing digits of her clock radio, the bottle of pills atop her nightstand.

THE COVER OF A GRAMMAR BOOK

The book's cover is the German flag: three horizontal stripes, black, red and yellow. In the red stripe are the words *Sprechen Sie Deutsch?* The colours are glossy. The book looks new despite a gouge hacked into the red stripe. Grey-brown pulp pokes out. As Amy fingers the pulp, she pictures Thomas deflecting a bullet with his grammar book. My hero, she thinks, the sad irony pinching her face and gunning her heart.

Before the shootings, Amy hadn't even known Thomas was enrolled in German class. After all, German was his mother tongue. He took the class on the sly to boost his grade point average, even flubbing answers so the professor wouldn't twig to his fluency.

By the time the shootings started, Thomas's grammar book was no longer in room 523. It was tucked under his arm as he hurried along the hallway, down the stairs and out of Robertson Hall. One guy from the class pulled a fire alarm. Another called 911. As for Thomas, he stepped around students as they sat on the campus lawn, sunning themselves on an Indian summer day. When he reached the edge of campus, he ran. He ran all the way home to Amy.

Amy didn't hear him come in. She was in her workshop, sketching designs for the dog boots she sells to pet shops. A thud from the living room jolted her. "Bugaboo," she called out. She peeked down the hall. There was Thomas, sitting on the futon couch in front of the steamer trunk they used as a coffee table. "Was yoga cancelled?" she asked, since that was where he supposedly spent Wednesday mornings. No answer. On the steamer trunk, beside some of her boot-making tools, lay a textbook. He was staring at this book.

"What's wrong, love?"

His Bob Marley T-shirt was speckled with sweat. His forehead too. He looked up, face contorted, lips quivering. He exhaled hard. Then he grabbed an awl, raised it above the book, and drove it straight down.

Amy's heart beat in her ears.

Days later, her heart is still in her ears. *Sprechen Sie Deutsch?* is splayed out on her drafting table. She has just amputated its cover with an exacto knife. As she picks at the gouge in the cover, she thinks of bullet holes, of having one in her chest as she thrashes on the floor of room 523. She could have been one of the eight.

She damn well could have been. All those times she promised Thomas's mother she'd learn more German than just *Gesundheit*.

She takes her awl and pokes it all the way through the gouge in the grammar book. Then she holds the book's cover to one eye and peers through the hole. She homes in on Thomas's back as he stumbles in a sleeping-pill stupor down the hall to the bathroom.

"Freeze," she says, "or I'll shoot."

Thomas is too far away to hear.

THE BACK OF AN ENVELOPE

Thomas sits on a stool in the middle of the kitchen. He's wearing cut-off jeans and, over his bare shoulders, two green garbage bags taped together like a flimsy sandwich board. With her fabric scissors, Amy has snipped off his dreadlocks, which now lie at her feet like sections of rope. As she finishes clipping around his ears, he says, "I wonder who's on that envelope."

Every day, she spoon-feeds him a few details from the newspaper articles he can't bring himself to read. Today *The Petertown Examiner* reported that Buddy MacDonald (or "the Silencer" as the press has dubbed him) left no suicide note. While searching his apartment, though, the police did come across a list of names on an envelope. A hit list. These names are of local women, all fairly prominent. "Leading lights" is how the police chief put it, although he wouldn't divulge exactly which leading lights Buddy wanted extinguished.

Amy goes to the sink, snaps on a pair of plastic gloves and shakes a bottle of hair dye. Thomas, meanwhile, picks up a pen and begins writing on the back of their unopened phone bill. She watches him. With short hair, his eyes look smaller, more wizened, and his forehead looks as square and white as a slice of sandwich bread. Amy wonders whether she's the only person who knows he was in that German class. The police haven't called. When their friends phone, she feeds them a story about Thomas visiting his sick mother in Montreal.

He hasn't ventured outdoors since the shootings ten days ago, but there will be a memorial march this weekend and she wants them both to be there. At first, he vetoed the idea: he's afraid of running into "the others," meaning his classmates from room 523—the two women who survived, the four guys who fled. She suggested he go incognito: sunglasses, no dreadlocks, brown hair. A new man.

When the dye is ready, she lathers the soapy mix into his hair. "Let's play a game," he says, tapping the phone bill against his knee. "I give you clues and you tell me which famous Petertown woman is on the back of my envelope."

"I don't want to play games."

She yanks off the plastic gloves and chucks them into the sink.

He grabs a grapefruit from a fruit bowl and shot-puts it into the living room. "She really throws her weight around," he says.

She stares at this boy with his garbage-bag apron and foamy ammonia head. She wants to hug him close; she wants to slap him hard. Finally, she says, "Olympic bronze medallist Becky Pepper."

"Bingo." A devious smirk cocks up one side of his mouth.

She plays along because they both have a warped sense of humour and this game feels restorative, although a bit painful, like blood flowing back into frostbitten toes. She plays along because she wants to hear him talking again after a week of his mumbling little more than "yep" and "nope."

For his next clue, he holds out his arm and pretends to saw it with a long breadknife.

"Violinist Margaret O'Reilly."

Other names on his envelope belong to a police officer, a novelist, an abortionist, an alderwoman and a country singer. After she guesses each woman, he strikes the name off his list.

In search of his final clue, he heads into the workshop, Bugaboo at his heels. She settles down on the couch, thankful for this momentary let-up in their storm, till he returns with colourful dog booties, her DogPoz, stuck on the ends of his fingers. He straddles her lap and taps her head and face with the boots. She closes her eyes, endures the tiny kicks. Finally she hisses, "Quit it!"

He lowers his hands.

"I'm no leading light," she says.

A treacherous look in his eye, he flicks off the booties and snatches a framed newspaper article hanging on the wall above the couch. "Amy Hamilton," he reads, "an up-and-coming businesswoman with a go-getter attitude." She shoves him backwards into the steamer trunk and wrests the frame away. How unhinged he looks, the dye dribbling down his forehead, his garbage bags askew.

She goes into her workshop and slams the door, locks it.

The day *The Petertown Examiner* ran "A Cobbler for Canines" on the front page, she felt such a balloon of elation. Thomas was so proud he yelled, he hooted, he went right out and had the article and its photograph matted and framed.

Now she stares into the face of the girl in the photograph. There she is, beaming behind Bugaboo, who offers a booted paw to the camera. She sees her blithe smile and imagines Buddy MacDonald, highlighter in hand, ringing her face in yellow.

"Bud MacDonald had a list, ee-eye ee-eye-oh," Thomas yells from the living room, "and on his list he had some gals, ee-eye ee-eye-oh. With a pow pow here and a pow pow there, here a pow, there a pow, everywhere a pow pow!"

The air sweeps from her lungs. Sweeps back in.

"Shut up!" she screams.

"Ee-eye ee-eye-oh—"

"Shut up!"

He's at the door, shaking the knob.

"A pow pow here and a pow pow there—"

Her anger is an awl through her chest.

"Piss off, you fucking coward!"

She has said it. What she knows he's wanted her to say all along. What she has felt. A sick, wavering, guilty feeling.

He stops shaking the knob.

Silence.

Eight women shot, and all the papers talk about is Buddy. Was he beaten with a yardstick as a child whenever he wet the bed? Was he a model employee at the paint shop where he worked? As a man, was he an aberration or the Hyde hidden in every Jekyll?

Her own man is on the floor now, his shadow edging under the door. The sounds he's making—short, sharp coughs—she recognizes as sobs. She shuffles to the door, opens it, kneels. He's on his side, his face planted in the crook of his arm. His front garbage bag is gone, but the back bag remains taped to his shoulders, a superhero's cape. Bugaboo licks his hand while Amy strokes his chest and plucks away stray snips of hair. So this is a man, she thinks numbly. When there's a lull in his crying, she whispers, "We've got to rinse your head, love, or your scalp will stain." She helps him up. The envelope drops from his back pocket. She sees her name. The only one without a strike through it.

EXCERPTS FROM NEWSPAPER PROFILES

Heidi mastered French's pluperfect, Spanish's imperfect and German's future perfect, but her favourite mood was the subjunctive. "It conjures up our wishes and desires," she would tell her students, "our fears and possibilities."

Her friends say that Louise often tried signing them up as volunteers for the Meals on Wheels program she helped run.

Tamara planned to become an accountant but was also toying with the idea of writing detective novels featuring a female private eye.

Mimi acted as a kind of resident therapist at her dorm. If a girl had a problem, she'd stop by Mimi's room. Her dormmates made her a sign to hang on the door when she wanted peace and quiet. She rarely used that sign, but it hangs there now. It reads, THE DOCTOR IS OUT.

Susan handled publicity for the local punk band Wuzzy and was often found in the mosh pit during the group's concerts.

A fan of Frida Kahlo, Vera painted self-portraits. Her younger brother has hung a dozen of these works on a wall in the family's den.

———

Cynthia plans to return to the Magdalen Islands when she has recovered. What she misses most about her tiny island home is the endless horizon. "Everywhere you look, there it is—infinity."

Despite her ordeal, Myuko has decided against returning to Tokyo. "Most people here are good people," she says. "Very, very good."

A DOUBLE LOOP OF RIBBON

Everywhere Amy looks, there it is—infinity.

A ribbon looped twice into a figure eight is being pinned to Thomas's sweatshirt. The ribbon is deep purple, the university's official colour. "You wear it on its side," says a girl with a pierced eyebrow as she adjusts Thomas's ribbon. "Like the infinity symbol."

"Doesn't she get one?" Thomas asks, nodding toward Amy.

"Only the guys," says the girl, who then, with her canvas purse full of pins and ribbons, drifts off through the crowd on the lookout for other ribbonless men.

"Infinity is the theme of the march," explains Amy. "Why?"

"Something to do with remembering the dead for eternity." She leaves out how men are also meant to reflect on the infinite number of women whose lives they've snuffed out.

It's mid-October. The sun is shining, but the ground is muddy from an overnight rainfall—hence the boots, the lighter fall model, that Bugaboo is wearing. Amy and Thomas are in Davies Park with two thousand other students, a good chunk of Scott University's student body. Despite the crowd, people are subdued. Amy sees a few girls weeping quietly and guys hugging the way guys do, two quick slaps on the back.

Under his mirrored sunglasses, Thomas's eyes are bloodshot, not from crying but from the pot he smoked to muster the nerve to go outside. Lately, Amy has barely been out either, other than to scoot to the store or to walk Bugaboo in the woods behind their apartment. She tugs on the dog's leash now to draw the animal closer, but Thomas, she feels, is the one who needs leashing: he keeps wandering off, craning his neck in search of her, and then scurrying back.

"You okay, love?"

He nods absently.

The march is to begin in fifteen minutes. It will be a silent march attended only by students from Scott University. They'll walk out of the park and, accompanied by a police escort, follow George Street past the downtown core, with its small shops tidily arranged like canisters of coffee, sugar, flour and tea. They'll then head north, past the library and petting zoo, and on to the subdivision where Amy and Thomas live, and finally up the road to the university campus. People from Amy's town, her parents and little brother among them, will line the sidewalks all the way, as will journalists from across the country and beyond.

A volunteer with a reddish goatee approaches Amy. "Would you like to carry a sign?" The young man is clutching a half-dozen placards, each bearing a blown-up photograph of one of the women killed.

Amy holds up Bugaboo's leash. "I've got my hands full." The dog sniffs the volunteer's muddy shoes.

"I'll take one," Thomas says.

"No can do," the volunteer replies. "The guys get the ribbons, the girls get the signs."

"Just give me a sign, man." Thomas grabs the sign displaying the Meals on Wheels girl. The volunteer pulls the sign back.

"I said you can't have one."

"Fuck you, asshole!"

"Take a pill, bud," the volunteer says, hurrying off.

"I already did," Thomas yells. "And don't call me Bud!"

People stare.

"Real cool," Amy snaps.

"Well, what's with the boy-gets-this, girl-gets-that crap. What's with rules when this whole fucking horror is, like, so . . . *unruly*?"

In his sunglasses, Amy sees herself, her fatigue warped into a jolly clown face by the funhouse mirrors of the lenses. She glances away and scans the crowd, recognizing a bald, furrowed head, the reporter who interviewed her about DogPoz. He's speaking to three girls. She turns away. She doesn't want to talk to him. He'd ask, "What are you feeling?" and she'd stare at the faces of the dead women bobbing over the heads of the crowd and say, "Relief." Relief as potent as guilt. Relief that no one is waving a sign with her face on it. Or with Thomas's.

The march begins. On the long walk to the university, Amy endures the silence by counting the number of fallen purple ribbons, muddied and trampled, that litter the way.

AN EXCERPT FROM AN ENCYCLOPEDIA ENTRY

The term "silencer" is somewhat of a misnomer, as gunshots cannot be truly silenced, but merely suppressed.

A JAPANESE CHARACTER

A Japanese girl is sitting under a pine tree. She wears a fuzzy cardigan sweater, a crisp white shirt and capri pants. A leather-bound notebook is on her lap, and her felt pen hovers over the page as she gathers her thoughts.

Despite his sunglasses, Amy can tell Thomas is staring.

The girl looks past them to the crowd on the football field, where students are filling the bleachers in preparation for the upcoming speeches. The silent march has ended here, just around the corner from Robertson Hall.

"I have to talk to her," he says.

"You can't. You're incognito, remember."

He slips off his sunglasses. "Don't do it," she says. "Chrissakes, Tom, you don't need to." He'll make things worse. Their friends might see him and think he's comforting a survivor. "That's just like Thomas," they'll say, and, though her face will burn, she won't blurt the truth.

He walks away, and she watches him interrupt the girl, whose name, she recalls from the newspaper, is Myuko. Myuko looks up, puzzled, and then smiles and with two fingers pantomimes scissors across her bangs. Thomas sits on the grass. Amy watches them talk. He has his demons to grapple with, she tells herself. They don't involve her. Myuko and Thomas are pink and purple stick figures on a diagram, whereas she is a shadowy grey bystander. Still, when Bugaboo pulls on the leash, draws her toward that pine tree, she doesn't resist.

Bugaboo scampers to Thomas and noses him in the ear. "A dog in go-go boots," Myuko says. She has a fleshy mole on her upper lip and faint eyebrows like a pair of smudged thumbprints. Thomas introduces Amy and the dog. Amy sits on the damp yellowing grass, and the three of them pretend to be absorbed by Bugaboo gnawing a pine cone, until Myuko mentions Cynthia, their classmate who's still in the hospital.

"She needs plastic surgery on her cheek," Myuko says, touching her own cheek. "So she jokes, why not get a nose job at the same time?"

Thomas and Amy smile.

"Have you been to see her?" Myuko asks Thomas. Amy begins to say that Thomas was out of town all week, but he cuts her off.

"I'll go tomorrow."

The newspaper said Myuko escaped with a flesh wound, and Amy wonders where underneath the girl's clothing that wound is. She stares. When Myuko catches her eye, she quickly looks away. She glances at the columns of Japanese characters filling the pages of Myuko's notebook.

"Are you keeping a diary?" Amy asks.

"Very healing." Myuko pats the pages. "You keep one?"

"Amy keeps scrapbooks," Thomas says.

"Mementoes, keepsakes, that kind of thing," Amy says. She attempted a diary in high school but found her entries never captured the intricacy of her feelings. Her words simply toddled across the page like a string of daycare tots, infantile and uncoordinated. In contrast, the objects in her scrapbooks conjure up a spectrum of emotions and memories.

Thomas peers at Myuko's notebook. "I wish I could write like that."

"Maybe you can study Japanese," Amy says, "after you've learned German." Thomas blinks fast, won't look at her, and she regrets her jab.

Myuko turns to a blank page in her diary and draws a large Japanese character, a blend of sabre-like dashes and strokes in black ink. She rips the page out and lays it on the grass between them.

"What does it mean?" Thomas asks.

"*Hyo,*" Myuko says. "That means big cat. The closest kanji to cheetah."

"You know Thomas's nickname?" Amy says.

"*Der Gepard,*" Myuko says. "And he knows mine."

"*Die Sonnenblume,*" Thomas says. "The sunflower." He explains that Heidi, their professor, had them choose German nicknames.

"Heidi was crazy lady," Myuko adds. "She said language is a virus from outer space." Myuko inhales sharply and then presses the heels of her palms into her eyes. "Poor *Glocke* and *Taube* and . . . and . . ."

"*Hündin und Giraffe und Apfelsine,*" Thomas finishes.

He leans into Myuko till the two of them are hugging, faces tucked into shoulders. Silent. Amy puts one hand on Thomas's back, the other gingerly on Myuko's back. She feels the heaving of their breath. She feels the heaving of her own. She glances down. On the grass, between the three of them, lies the big cat. Amy tries to make out a cheetah in the random lines and dashes, but the character could be anything. An elephant, a tulip. Or something less easy to define. Rage, love, shame, forgiveness. Any of these things.

Or all of them at once.

THE BUTTERFLY BOX

I REMEMBER POSING for my father. The first time, I was five years old.

That afternoon, my mother had whirled our dachs-hund's food bowl across the kitchen, clipping my father on the chin. Then she'd crammed her suitcases into her Rambler and squealed off down the street. When Fred slunk out of his studio, I was making thumbprints in the gobs of Alpo on the linoleum. He towelled off my hands and plunked me down on the chesterfield.

He didn't lie to me. He didn't say, "She'll be back."

He hardly spoke a word. He simply went to get his sketchpad so he could capture my look of bewilderment.

Skip ahead seventeen years to the opening night of Fred's retrospective. Here I am again, posing. At one time, I could hold a pose for hours on end. But tonight I already have a crick in my neck and pins and needles in my legs.

I'm posing downtown in the display window at the Nurani Art Gallery. It was the Curator's idea to place my old bed, our tiffany floor lamp and our chipped wooden armoire in the window just as they're arranged in one of Fred's paintings.

We're recapturing a moment, or so said the Curator. "A moment of what?" I asked.

"That's for you to decide," he answered. "After all, it's your retrospective, too."

I sit cross-legged on the bed with a shallow glass-lid case in my lap. Pinned inside the case is *Morpho peleides.* A Blue Morpho. One of the dozens of butterflies I collected as a kid.

My eyes drift toward a sign hanging in the display window. The sign faces outward so its words appear to people passing in the street. It says: FRED ROBERTSON, 1997, *The Butterfly Box.*

To me it reads like an epitaph.

———

I live in the town of Hammond, which isn't far from the city—just a hop, skip and a dump, as Fred was fond of saying. Mine is that two-storey brick home with the thicket of peeling birch trees out front and a porch so sunken it seems to smile at you from the street.

The day Fred sketched out *The Butterfly Box*, I was sixteen, scrawny as a Giacometti sculpture. My father sat me down on my bed. He straightened my shoulders and raked the bangs from my forehead.

He sat across from me in his tie and blazer and polished oxblood shoes. His sketching clothes. You'd have thought he was making his living as a banker instead of as an artist and teacher.

As I watched his pencil figure-skate across the sketchpad, I began daydreaming of a trek we'd taken to the Mexican tropics the summer before. It was there I'd captured the Blue Morpho, the iridescent brooch inside the box in my lap.

"Hey, Jack," Fred whispered. "Stop your fidgeting." I was stock-still. It was our running joke: he knew his fingers would cramp up before I'd lose a pose.

"Want to know how I'd draw?" I asked.

"Enlighten me." His thumb smudged graphite across the page.

I told him I'd take a photograph of an image and then trace a grid over top, with boxes one inch by one inch. In my sketchpad, I'd draw another grid with boxes two inches by two inches. Using the grid lines as my guide, I'd clone the image—the same but bigger.

Fred ping-ponged his eyes between me and his sketchpad. "Wouldn't you be boxing yourself in?"

Well, that was the idea.

A few days later, I tried my technique. I pulled out a *National Geographic* with an article on the Blue Morpho. I tore out a full-page photograph and traced my grid over top. On watercolour paper, I duplicated *Morpho peleides,* erased the grid lines, and then painted the butterfly wings blue.

"What do you think?"

"Pretty good," Fred replied.

I studied my butterfly. It looked so two-dimensional: flat, lifeless. But then Fred placed it against the sunny window in his studio and the butterfly lit up like stained glass. He bent the sides of the sketch back and forth till the Morpho fluttered its wings and took flight.

"Ollie-Ollie-oxen-free."

I look up and see the Curator's man-in-the-moon face poking through the curtain that hems in the back of the window display.

"Excuse me?"

The Curator's wire Ben Franklin glasses hop down his nose. "I mean you can come out now."

I met the Curator at Fred's first show at the Nurani. I was twelve and had called him the Mortician because we'd just attended my great-aunt's funeral the week before. Honest mistake, Fred admitted. They both deal in the remains of the dead.

The Curator steps into the display window and lowers his rump onto the bed. He sighs wistfully.

"Jack, your father's work is a wonderful empirical means of suspending the flow of time."

This is how the art world sweet-talks.

"Fred's with us," says the Curator. His breath has the vernissage smell of Camembert cheese and green grapes. "He's thankful so many people are here admiring his work."

Many of the guests are probably ticked off they didn't buy sooner, before the value shot up.

The Curator tugs a handkerchief from his blazer pocket and cleans his glasses as people pass in the street. Three Girl Scouts plaster themselves against the window like gecko lizards.

The Curator pats my hand and stands up to go. "Maybe you'd prefer visiting the exhibition after everyone leaves."

I nod.

The only thing better than an art exhibit without the people is an art exhibit without the art.

In the summertime, Fred had a break from the modern art classes he taught at Perkin College. He'd spend his days hidden away in his studio, a hump-like addition on the back of the house that we called Quasimodo.

One summer day, I bicycled home after my shift at Critters, the local pet shop, and joined Fred in the studio.

"Hey, you're getting musty, man," I said. "You need an airing."

He glanced up, foggy-eyed, from a canvas. Beside him, his tubes of paint were queued up by hue.

"How about a walk?" I asked. Alice, our arthritic dachshund, click-clacked toward me across the hardwood floor.

"Maybe later."

"Listen, you haven't been outside in three days. You haven't spoken to a soul but me in two weeks."

"A lecture on socializing from a guy whose best friend is a Red Admiral butterfly."

Ignoring this, I scooped up Alice in my arms. "Look what our daddy has painted today," I said in a needling baby voice. I pointed the dog's snout toward the canvas. "Look at that pretty lady. Such a pretty lady for daddy."

Fred sighed and laid his brush down.

We ended up walking to Necropolis, the name he'd given to the cemetery in town. We sat down on the graves, Fred beside Cordelia Feltwell's tombstone (REMEMBER ME IS ALL I ASK) and me beside George Kingston Sr.'s (TO LOVE IS TO BURY). Willow trees swayed in the breeze like giant hula dancers.

"Feeling loquacious, Jack?" Fred wanted me to talk.

"Guess how Cordelia died," I said after a moment. "One evening the old lush sets up the blender on the side of the tub. She wants to mix up daiquiris while soaking in her bubble bath. After her third drink, she knocks the blender into the water, creates a new cocktail—a Cordelia cordial."

Fred rolled his eyes and mouthed a Camel from his cigarette pack.

"Then there's George Kingston." I nodded toward the tombstone, with its crumbling parade of angels. "He's a Mormon minister preaching polygamy. That is, till his two wives fall for each other, ditch him and make a killing co-inventing the plastic nibs on the end of shoelaces. The envy does him in."

Fred scratched his beard. "You know, Jack, they can do wonders today with electroshock." He dragged on his Camel and eyed Alice, who was yapping at a cater-pillar crawling up Cordelia's tombstone. I threw a stick across the graveyard, and Alice hobbled after it. Then I placed my finger in the caterpillar's path. It stepped aboard. From the blond punk-rock spikes on its back, I could tell it would metamorphose into *Colias croceus*. A Clouded Yellow.

"You know, Fred, the ancient Greeks believed that after death the soul flew from the body as a butterfly."

Fred stuck his face up close to my outstretched hand. He dragged on his cigarette and puffed a whiff of smoke at the caterpillar. It rolled up like a sleeping bag.

How many stories like this make up a retrospective?

Sitting mannequin-stiff on my bed, I watch the guests drift out of the art gallery. Some stop and point or greet me with little Queen Elizabeth waves.

From behind the curtain comes the Curator's voice. "Is our jack-in-the-box ready to take a look around?"

By the time I turned thirteen, I'd become an expert on the Canadian realists. Or so I believed. On a trip to the National Gallery in Ottawa, I walked past their paint-ings, announcing "Mary Pratt" or "Hugh MacKenzie" or "Ken Danby." But I barely looked at their works. "Slow down," Fred ordered, pinching the nape of my neck. He told me to pick a canvas and study it till I had something more intelligent to say than the artist's name.

"Contemplate and appreciate," he said.

So I stewed on a bench in front of an Alex Colville, a painting of a young man target shooting with his father. The younger man, standing in the foreground, was square-jawed and valiant, his pistol aimed confidently at a target outside the frame. His jowly father stood in the background, a pair of binoculars pressed against his eyes.

I tried thinking up clever things to say about brush strokes and the play of light and dark. But everything I came up with sounded pre-chewed by Fred. So in the end, I invented a story about the two characters in the painting. Long-brewing animosity. A quarrel over shooting technique. The son turning on his father. The pistol firing by accident. Blood spurting from a wound.

My aim was to rile Fred up.

A while later my father returned to the exhibit hall where I was still "contemplating." Fred sat. I spoke. He listened. He grinned. When I finished, he said, "Every picture tells a story, eh, Jack?"

He did not look riled up. He rubbed the back of my neck, which still smarted from being pinched.

I pushed his hand away. At that moment, a group of visitors came into the exhibit hall and glanced at Fred and me. I wondered what story our picture told.

Goosepimply ominous—that's how one reviewer described Fred's work. My father liked that. He wanted his paintings to be snapshots of the windless calm before an earthquake hits.

As I walk into the exhibit hall, that's the calm I feel. The hall is long and narrow, with wooden floor slats that seem to converge at its far end. Fred's canvases are hung on the walls in clusters.

In *Barbershop,* a man draped in a sheet sits waiting for a trim. Next to him, a tangle of scissors soak in a jar. In *Push Me Higher,* a barefoot woman with a lopsided smile sits on a playground swing.

What I like is looking at Fred's paintings up close. So close, say, that the hand gripping that playground swing bursts into a dapple of yellows and oranges and licks of navy.

The woman on the swing is Judy. She was my boss at Critters and, for a few months, Fred's girlfriend and muse. In fact, all of my father's muses grace the paintings hung around the hall. There's Samantha with her Dada tattoos, including a furry teacup in her armpit. On the far wall is Teresa, a potter from

Mexico who taught me to differentiate smells of clay. Next to her, we have Diane, a cookbook writer who put Fred and me on a vegan diet that left us lactose intolerant. None of these women remained in the picture very long. The day Diane dumped my father, she said that if her love life were a meal Fred would be Melba toast—a flat, tasteless appetizer.

So, with the muses always disappearing, who stepped in to pose when it came time to paint? The arms cradling that jug of milk in *Elimination Diet,* the shoulder blade under that tattoo in *Indelible Ink,* those strained calves, the nape of that neck, even the hand grasping the playground swing. Scattered all over the room are pieces of me.

In the last canvas I come to, these pieces merge. There I am, sitting on my bed, my head cocked sideways. In my lap is the butterfly box. I tilt it up, but the glass front of the box acts as a mirror so that what appears is not a Red Admiral or a Clouded Yellow or a Blue Morpho. What appears is the reflected face of the artist staring back. My father, transfixed by his own reflection.

I walk out of the hall and come face to face with a publicity poster for the exhibit. It's Fred's profile, with his name printed across the bottom. Underneath his name is a date: *1948–*   . I stare at this date. A prickly blush creeps across my face as I realize how much I want that empty space filled.

An autumn afternoon a year and eleven months ago. Fred and I were lazing in the backyard on what I jokingly called our chaises longues. I was reading a book on ferret breeding. Fred was sulking through a funk. The reason? Maybe a spat with a muse, a stack of student papers to mark, a canvas gone awry.

"Robertson's blue period, I presume," I mumbled.

He turned away from me in his lawn chair. A handful of change spilled from the pocket of his smock and jingled onto the patio.

"I'll head inside and make supper," I said and put my book down. I planned to make tacos and cornbread, Fred's favourites. "You stay outside awhile. You need the fresh air."

"For Christ's sake," Fred snapped. "You're the opposite of a mamma's boy. You're a boy mamma. You sure I don't need a sweater in case it turns cold?"

I scowled at him and went inside. In the kitchen, I tore apart a head of lettuce. I grated the cheddar cheese with such force I decapitated a wart on my thumb. Yet by the time the cornbread was baked, wouldn't you know I was whistling along to the oldies station.

The oven had heated the kitchen up, and so I went

to the back window and hoisted it open. Across the lawn I could see Fred. He was kneeling on the ground beside a grove of birch trees. He was looking straight at me through the window.

I waved and thought, beautiful composition–the shimmering grass, the still trees, Fred in his paint-speckled smock. Then I noticed his mouth. It was opening and closing soundlessly like the puffer fish in their tanks at the pet shop.

In two seconds, I was out the door, but already he was face down in the grass.

Before heading home, I climb back into the display window to pick up the butterfly box. I sit down on the bed and consider slipping between the covers and spending the night.

The Blue Morpho looks up at me, its wings flaring like a blowtorch flame.

"Why not go see him tonight?" I imagine it saying. "You hardly ever drop by anymore."

In the corridor, I pass an empty stretcher and order-lies in running shoes. It's the same toothpaste-coloured corridor I've walked down countless times before. When I reach his room, I stop, glance through the window and drum my fingers against the glass.

I see the monitor with the zigzagging line, like a seismograph measuring aftershocks. I see the plastic tubing and respirator. I open the door, walk into his room. I step up close. Close enough to see the capillaries in his earlobe, the flick of an eyelid, the gentle rising of his chest.

When you die and are put into the ground, your fingernails continue to grow. And so do his. So I tug open the drawer of the bedside table and fish around for the clipper. Then I pick up his hand and feel its warmth. One by one, I clip his nails and heap the little crescent moons into a pile on his chest.

When I'm finished, I draw up a chair and sit. I ask him questions—"Any news from Cordelia Feltwell?"—and then make up his replies as the IV drips into a vein in his wrist.

Later a nurse taps a knuckle against the window. She points to her wristwatch: visiting hours are over.

I stand, stretch, and then bend over the bed to pull the blanket up. Fred's arm jumps and knocks my hand away. It's only a spasm.

"Stop your fidgeting," I say.

I'd netted the Blue Morpho along a dirt road bordered by palm trees. It was late summer, and Fred and I were in Mexico on the northern edge of the tropics. From the road, we could hear the roaring waterfall, El Salto.

My father was engrossed by the Blue Morpho as it flitted around the killing jar, its wings fracturing and reflecting the sunlight. To asphyxiate the butterfly, I needed to add a few drops of ethyl acetate to the jar. Yet whenever I made a move to, Fred stopped me.

"He's not ready to go," Fred insisted.

After fifteen minutes of this, I got fed up. "Enough contemplation," I said. Then I introduced the poison.

FUNNY WEIRD OR FUNNY HA HA?

I LOVED LUCY, that loopy redhead with the Silly Putty face. When I was a girl, about ten years old, I'd watch the reruns of her show and howl. Practically pee on my mother's throw rug in front of the TV. "Peggy," my mother would call out from the kitchen, "restrain yourself." Later, in my bedroom mirror, I'd practise my Lucy faces. Her bug-eyed surprise. Her clownish smile. Also her blubbering *Wahhhhhh!* when she was scolded by long-suffering Ricky Ricardo.

In my favourite episode, Lucy auditioned for a TV

commercial plugging a vitamin tonic. "Are you run-down and listless? Are you unpopular?" Lucy recited as the tonic's spokesmodel. "The answer to all your problems, friends, is in this little bottle: Vitameatavegamin." She poured a spoonful of the tonic and swallowed the stuff, her face twisting from its terrible taste. Vitameatavegamin contained twenty-three percent alcohol, and so, after several run-throughs of the commercial, Lucy was sloshed. She tripped over the product's name, flubbed her lines. Too tipsy to pour the tonic onto her spoon, she downed it straight from the bottle like a Bowery bum.

The studio audience and I howled.

"Restraint," my mother cried.

Later I put on that sketch for my parents and little sister, Elaine. I stood behind a card table, holding an old bottle of cough syrup filled with apple juice. Behind me, taped to my bedroom wall, was a poster I'd drawn of a bottle of Vitameatavegamin with its slogan DRINK YOUR WAY TO HEALTH!

"Friends, with Vita-*vomit*-vegamin," I slurred, "you'll never be un*poop*ular again." I crossed my eyes and chug-a-lugged the tonic.

My father hooted, my sister giggled, my mother even cracked a smile. Afterwards, my father patted me on the shoulder, saying, "You slay me, kid."

I had the red hair. I had the rubber face. My middle name was even Lucille. I was sure I'd grow up to be a comedienne.

My late husband, Carl, used to say that a cucumber could be turned into a pickle, but a pickle could never be changed back into a cucumber. "Once pickled, you stay pickled," he'd say, "even if you're no longer soaking in your favourite vinegar." (My favourite vinegar was a Chablis Drouhin, a Chardonnay with a hint of almond and honey.)

Carl shared my weird sense of humour. For instance, when our son, Max, was born, he hung an Edward Gorey poster beside Max's crib. The poster consisted of comical pen drawings of twenty-six little kids representing the letters of the alphabet. Each kid was killed in a bizarre way. "K is for Kate who was struck with an axe. L is for Leo who swallowed some tacks."

Carl died in an unusual way: he was lining up a shot during a curling championship when a blood vessel burst in his thalamus. After his death, "C is for Carl who died on the curling rink" kept running through my head. In the end, I had his ashes placed in a hollowed-out curling stone. A lovely grey-blue stone.

I'm looking for that stone now.

This morning, I've moved into a new home, a condominium apartment on the edge of Parc Lafontaine. The movers have just left, and I'm wandering around the piles of boxes. I have time to sort through them: I've taken five weeks off from the clinic where I work as a dermatologist. I find Carl's box (the box my old juice extractor came in) on my kitchen cupboard. I open the box, fish through the foam peanuts and pull out the curling stone by its curved handle.

"Welcome home, Carl."

I talk to Carl all the time, both out loud and in my head. We have conversations insofar as I know how he'd respond to anything I say or do. Some people may think chatting with your dead husband is maudlin or the premise of a hokey Hollywood movie. But screw them. I'll do what I want.

With the counters strewn with my belongings, I set the stone down on a burner on the stove.

Teapot by Marcel Duchamp, Carl says.

I smile at that one. But then my radio plays Nina Simone's *"Ne me quitte pas"* and I'm no longer smiling.

I've never lived alone. Though I'm basically an introvert, I'm an introvert who has trouble being by herself. All my life I've lived with others: my family, roommates in university, then Carl (we married young) and Max.

Max. Max-a-Million. Moody Max (although at nineteen years old, how could he be otherwise?). A month ago, he crammed his belongings into my old Civic, his going-away present, and drove off to Boston, where he starts university in the fall.

God, I miss my kid. To cheer me up, Carl does his Nina Simone imitation. In a fake throaty rage, he sings, *Don't you leave me now. Or else I'll whinge and whine. I'll booze it up. I'll binge on wine. Don't you leave me now. Don't you leave me now.*

"I miss you, too, you son of a bitch."

I miss the stupidest things. For example, there was this thing Carl did. He had allergies—to dust, pollen, our old cat—and he'd massage his neck and Adam's apple to coax the post-nasal drip down his throat. The whole routine reminded me of a blue heron swallowing a fish.

You miss my post-nasal drip? Carl is aghast. *How romantic! That's like missing the pee stains on my boxers.*

I give Carl the nickel tour of our new home, pointing out the features he'd approve of. The oak mouldings. The crimson tiles on the kitchen wall. One perk of widowhood, I tell him, is the bedroom closet you no longer share.

I have a surprise for Carl. I carry the stone onto my fifth-floor balcony with its wrought-iron balustrade. Far down Amherst Street stands the Tour de l'Horloge, a clock tower near the river. Carl calls it Little Big Ben because the company that built the famous clock tower in London also worked on the Tour de l'Horloge.

Carl, Max and I used to picnic on a bench beside the tower. I'd make a quiche. Max would lob pastry crust at the seagulls. Carl would read a novel. We'd all watch the boats in the St. Lawrence River speed by.

I'd drink a glass of wine. Or two.

I go inside my apartment and set Carl down. I feel a familiar, clinging loneliness. Not a blanket or shroud of loneliness, but something thinner, tighter. A leotard of loneliness.

I close my eyes and there it is: a chilled Chablis Drouhin, beads of moisture dotting the bottle.

Tony the astronomer is talking about his rock bottom. He holds up a plastic model of the Earth, the size of a basketball, and jokes that he's Atlas, the Greek god. He is Greek (his name is actually Antonios) and hand-some, with his dark, bristly hair and intense brown eyes. On his forehead is one wavy wrinkle above two straight gouges, like the approximately-equal-to sign in math.

Tony says his rock bottom wasn't a traumatic event: he never smashed up his car, got thrown in jail or lost his job at the Planetarium.

"People at work didn't even know I drank," he says. "I was the classic high-functioning alcoholic." He separates the two halves of his model. The inside face of one half reveals different coloured rings surrounding a grey orb at the centre of the Earth.

"This is called the inner core," he says, pointing to the grey orb. "I needed to sink down through all my dirt and crust and mantle and shit till I got to my rocky inner core. The real me. Not the clown who made the kids at the Planetarium laugh, but the desperate guy who sat home every night sipping Smirnoff. A guy scared shitless. What was I so afraid of?"

He makes eye contact with the twenty of us gathered in the basement of the Atwater Library. I look him in the eye and then glance at his T-shirt: a cracked, leaky vodka bottle with the slogan ABSOLUT LUSH underneath.

"Maybe I was afraid of life."

I like Tony. After his wife left him recently, he let slip that he buys bars of her expensive goat-milk soap to shave with so that her scent lingers on his face all day. As a dermatologist and a widow, I could probably relate, he said. That's when I fessed up about the curling stone and my conversations with it. He understood perfectly. He said in all sincerity that he personally knew a lot of inanimate objects with more human personalities than many humans.

At the end of Tony's talk, people clap, and he asks, "Is there a doctor in the house?" because I'm up next.

I stand at the front like a stand-up comic.

The story I tell happened years ago. At the time, my sister owned a townhouse in the red-light district near the bus terminal. Elaine was away for the summer, and after work I'd often go water the flowers in her backyard. But I'd water more than her clematis: I'd buy a bottle of wine and gulp most of it down. I'd lie sozzled in her backyard till the fog began dissipating. Then I'd ride the metro home.

One night I drank the whole bottle and some of my sister's port. I passed out in the backyard under the ox-eye daisies, and my husband, sick with worry, found me there around midnight. Carl had to climb over a fence to get to me. By this time, I'd sobered up, although my brain felt like a bongo drum.

"You're overreacting," I told him, even though Carl wasn't reacting at all. He was dead silent.

As we left my sister's house, we saw a woman teetering on high heels on the front sidewalk. She stood under a street lamp. Other than her heels and a tiny purse slung over one shoulder, she was naked. Starkers. A big Rubenesque woman with heavy breasts. A woman high on something, a dopey grin on her face.

I went back inside to call 911. From the kitchen

window, I watched the woman wave at passing cars, whose drivers rubbernecked to stare. Carl pulled our picnic blanket from the trunk of our car and tried wrapping it around the woman. She slapped his hands away.

I thought, Clobber him, honey. I was still mad at his silent treatment.

Soon a cop car pulled up, and we watched awkwardly as the two officers wrestled the naked lady into the back seat. By this time, she was laughing. A crazed, busted-gut laugh. When she started urinating on the seat, my mother's voice came into my head: "Restrain yourself!" The cops cursed, and Carl handed over our picnic blanket to wipe down the woman and the car seat.

Later, on our drive home, I tried lightening the mood by telling my husband what the 911 operator had asked when I phoned. "The guy said, 'Could you describe the individual, ma'am?' And I said, 'Describe her? She's the only naked broad on the street. But if you have trouble picking her out, she's the one with the red purse.'"

The people at AA laugh. I tell them that Carl wouldn't laugh. He wouldn't even look at me. He glared straight ahead. Finally, he muttered, "A cautionary tale, Peg. A cautionary tale."

But it wasn't. Not for me. That naked lady wasn't a warning; she was a big relief. She confirmed what

I thought an addict was. Someone lurching out of control, demeaning herself in public. Probably scrambling her brains on heroin.

I wasn't that. I was a respected MD who'd just published a pioneering paper on rosacea. I never missed a day of work even during my worst discombobulating hangovers. So I had a bit too much wine on occasion. But a Château Montus, at twenty-five dollars a bottle, wasn't heroin.

My turn to look people in the eye: Wanda. Big lug Stan. Sweet Marie-Ève. Grandmotherly Huguette. Antonios the Greek. Ian and Michel and Donna and Stew and the rest.

"I was high up in the turret of the Château Montus, and that naked lady was lying at the bottom of the moat."

On a hot summer evening a week after my move, I'm sitting on my new balcony, ignoring all the boxes I've yet to unpack, all the furniture I've yet to arrange. My bare feet rest on the cool curling stone as I sip lemonade and read a book, an inside look at the *I Love Lucy* show. But the book I've bought to cheer me up is disheartening. In real life, Ricky was a womanizer and a cheat and Fred a mean-spirited drunk. Ethel struggled with soul-crushing despair and suicidal thoughts. Even Lucy said she was no comedienne: she could *play* funny but she was not naturally funny.

The lives of four unhappy dead people.

From under my feet, Carl says, *What is Pollyanna's epitaph?*

I'm glad I'm dead.

This was Carl's favourite joke. I almost engraved it on the curling stone, except our son wouldn't have found it funny. He's a serious kid, Max.

As if an umbilical phone cord connects Montreal to Boston, my phone rings and it's Max. I stretch the cord out to the balcony to talk. He asks how my move went. I say I fear for my mental stability after an entire day spent shopping for the perfect shelf liner.

He mutters something, but I can tell he's not really listening.

"Mom, I've had an accident."

My heart hiccups.

"Don't worry," he says. "It's just a mild concussion."

"*Just* a concussion," I yell. "What the hell happened?"

A skateboard mishap.

"I bet you weren't wearing a helmet. Damn it, Max. I bought you that helmet to wear, and I don't care if you think you look like a dork with it, you're gonna wear it. Did you lose consciousness? Because if you did, that's not a mild concussion, Max, that's a grade-three concussion. Did you go to Emergency?"

"I didn't pass out. I just felt dazed."

"You may have had a grade-two, Max! I want to speak to your doctor. I hope you had a CT."

In the background, his roommate, René-Louis Robidoux, is yelling, "Banana peel! Banana peel!"

"Banana peel?"

"Well, according to Ruby-Doo, the thing I hit before I wiped out was a smushed banana on the sidewalk."

I see my kid flying through the air. I hear Groucho Marx saying, "Time flies like an arrow. Fruit flies like a banana."

"I'm flying to Boston. I'm talking to your doctor."

"No, Ma, don't," Max pleads. "I'm fine. I've got a good doctor. Besides, Ruby-Doo's here to make sure I don't lapse into a coma."

"Don't even joke about that. And listen, Max. Promise you'll wear a helmet. Buy one you like and wear the damn thing. For Christ's sake, wear it all the time—even when you're making your bed or flossing your teeth."

After I hang up, Carl says, *Max has a tough noggin. Remember when he fell off his tricycle?*

I should be there. I'm a doctor.

You're a dermatologist, Peg. Max can call you if his pimples need squeezing.

Are you saying my kid doesn't need me?

Don't get all mawkish. And don't spend Saturday night alone. I don't like when you're lonely. Don't you bloody HALT on me.

HALT is AA-speak for: don't get too Hungry, too Angry, too Lonely, too Tired.

Go out. The comedy festival is on. Call up the Greek god and invite him along.

Tony is still pining over his ex-wife. He can't understand why she ditched him after he got sober.

Well, you have that in common. I did the same thing to you.

He did; he died.

With the windows left open, the doors in my apartment slam shut. You'd think I was still living with a fuming, door-slamming husband. "How ironic that in death you're a doorstop," I tell Carl, because the curling stone now holds my bedroom door open. Two weeks after my move, and I've accomplished little. I feel so heavy, as if my blood were gruel. Each day I manage this: one square of shelf liner cut out and pasted down in a kitchen cupboard. Meanwhile, all around me, cardboard boxes spit out my belongings.

Nights I sleep directly on my mattress, too sluggish to search for the fitted sheet; days I spend sitting in my bedroom doorway and leafing through old books.

Remember the earthquake back in the late eighties? You, me and little Max huddled in a doorway while the house swayed. For once it was the earth shaking that had you wobbly on your feet.

I flip through a book on the art nouveau buildings of Gaudi and then through the stories of Edgar Allan Poe. I haven't cracked these open in years. Why have I kept them? At AA, Tony claimed he tunnelled through his crust and mantle to reach his core. Maybe I have too much crap around me to find my core. After sifting through a pile of novels I'll never read again, I get an idea. I drag myself up, find a roll of paper towels and rip off three sheets. I write IN, OUT and MAX on the sheets before taping them to the walls in three corners of my living room.

For the next few days, I sort through my boxes, Carl egging me on. *You'll never use that juice extractor, Peg,* and so I toss it into my "out" corner. *With your red hair, that green sweater makes you look like a leprechaun.* Out goes the sweater. Out go my old watercolour set, my fax machine, throw pillows, three wristwatches, a Bundt cake pan, a desk fan, non-stick cookie sheets that stick every time, and on and on.

I can't put my in's away till I've thrown out my out's. Once my out pile has grown large enough, I load the junk into moving boxes, which I cart into the elevator and then heave into the Dumpster behind my building. Max's stuff goes into boxes that I drag to the storage locker in the basement.

I feel an urgency now: no time to recycle or call the United Way. *Is this what they call voluntary simplicity?* Carl asks. But this junking of my past feels as voluntary as breathing. Why do I have so many dishes when I abhor hosting dinner parties? Why do I have so many CDs when I only ever listen to that one jazz station? Within days, I've discarded two-thirds of my belongings. As for my plants, I can't bear to throw them in the Dumpster, so I cart them to Parc Lafontaine for strangers to adopt. A teak coffee table I abandon in an alleyway, along with a floor lamp. After four days of this, I scan my suddenly less cramped apartment and feel better. Lighter. I laugh, surprised at myself. What the hell am I doing?

From his doorway roost, Carl says, *You're reinventing yourself again. Wife, mother, doc, drunk, twelve-stepper, widow, nutso. Who will Peg be next?*

He's starting to sound like Poe's tell-tale heart.

Where do we go from here? he says. *What do we get rid of now?*

I eye the curling stone. Nudge it with my shoe.
You slay me, kid. What a comedienne!

I explain to the cabbie that for supper tonight I'm picnicking with my husband. I've made a leek quiche and a pound cake, I lie. Beside me on the back seat is a big picnic basket made of rattan. The cabbie, a man with a scaly, red dermatitis behind his ears, insists we should all spend more time with our loved ones. After he drops me off in the Old Port, I walk to the Quai de l'Horloge, which runs along the St. Lawrence River. I trudge along with my basket, thankful that the curling stone was hollowed out: a cremated husband is lighter than granite. At the end of the quay is Little Big Ben, the clock tower visible from my balcony. I sit on a bench. It's seven thirty in the evening, and the sky is blue bleeding into pink. Across the river on Île Sainte-Hélène, the roller coaster and other amusement-park rides blink their coloured lights. Over my head, seagulls caw. A young couple in matching bandanas stroll past hand in hand. "*Bonsoir*" they say to the nice middle-aged lady with a rattan basket at her feet.

My basket is rectangular and has a cover that flips open on either end like a car's trunk and hood. When the coast is clear, I open one side of the basket and pull out the curling stone. I stroke its surface.

The granite is called Blue Hone. It's quarried, if I remember correctly, in Scotland. When Carl died, Max was upset that I'd stopped up his father's ashes in a curling stone. Why not sprinkle them in a forest or a river the way normal people do? But I insisted on the curling stone. I wanted Carl around.

I wanted him around for the camaraderie.

But that's not all, is it?

The compassion he'd shown me.

There's more to it than that.

The memory of love.

What else?

I swat at my stupid tears.

You've stayed dry this long because of one thing.

One thing?

Me. My presence. My constant watch. I'm your rock.

My hand grabs the stone's handle. You prick, I think. You prick! I grip till my knuckles turn white. I squeeze till my hand weakens and I must let go.

I sit awhile and then finally flip open the other side of the rattan basket. Draped in a dish cloth is a bottle of Wolf Blass Gold Label Chardonnay 2003. In the pocket of my poncho is a corkscrew. I work the screw in; I slide the cork out. It makes a sound like a kiss. From the basket, I remove a wine glass wrapped in a hankie. I pour, twisting the bottle slightly so no wine spills.

I smell the wine first, the tiny hairs in my nostrils standing like hackles. I tilt the glass. The wine runs into my mouth, across my tongue, along my palate.

Warm pear. Golden apple. Narcissus. Vanilla.

How can a taste so sublime be wrong?

I proved you wrong, buster, I think. You're here and so is Wolf Blass.

Wolf sits on one side of me, Carl on the other.

Carl says nothing. His hateful silent treatment.

I drink two big glasses. I take my time. I enjoy them. I *so* enjoy them.

When the quay is empty of evening strollers, I grip the curling stone in one hand. In the other I clutch the neck of Wolf Blass. I walk to the railing. A few metres below, the green-black water laps against the concrete quay. I hold my husband and the half-empty bottle over the railing.

I fall off this quay, you fall off the wagon.

Too late, I think. I've already fallen.

My arms tremble. I let go.

When Wolf hits the water, Carl says, *Down now, Peg. You can put me down.* He's speaking as gently as you would to a woman on a ledge. Back over the railing comes my rock, the rock of Sisyphus.

———

When I'm packing Carl back into the picnic basket, he tells me we could both use a laugh. *The comedy festival is still on. Why don't we go? For old time's sake.* So I grab a cab to the Quartier latin, where the Just for Laughs festival is held. Saint-Denis Street is closed off. Drag queens wearing Marie Antoinette wigs lurch by on stilts. On a platform, a woman dressed as the Tin Man—with a funnel on her head and her face painted silver—stands motionless as if rusted solid. As I move through the crowd, I glimpse several of the festival's mascots, a green version of the Blue Meanie from *The Yellow Submarine.* Also on hand are acrobats, jugglers of china cups and the dreaded mime. At Théâtre Saint-Denis, the marquee advertises Andrea Martin's one-woman show, *The Lint Inside My Belly Button.* Every year, the festival holds a parade of identical twins, and many of them are out tonight. I spot little-boy twins, Asian twins, tattooed twins. What I'm looking for is an outdoor movie screen. I find it in an abandoned lot set up with rows of chairs.

Onscreen a cop in a squad car is signalling a driver over. To the woman glancing in her rear-view mirror, the cop looks normal. But I've seen this sketch. When the cop steps out of his car, he'll be wearing lace panties, a garter belt and black stockings. He'll sashay. The driver will bug out her eyes and the audience will roar.

———

Before Wolf Blass, one of the last drinks I had was at my sister's fortieth, a brunch organized in a Moroccan restaurant in Old Montreal. A kind, easygoing woman, Elaine has loads of friends and the place was packed, rai playing so loudly people had to shout to be heard. Since it was hard to talk, everyone got more liquored up than usual. Especially me. I eyed the bottles of wine. Whenever the Chardonnay dipped below three-quarters empty, I motioned to the waiter.

The floor show was a cross-eyed belly dancer with a horsey face and a frenetic jiggle. The boa she wore around her neck was a python. As she wiggled her stomach in her genie costume, I shouted in Carl's ear, "Barbara Eden on crack." He gave me a thin, mean smile and turned away. Barbara Eden tried to coax Carl into dancing with her and her snake, but he wouldn't budge. She wrapped a scarf around his head. I slapped the table in laughter and upended a bowl of couscous. My mother glowered.

At the end of the brunch, I hugged Elaine too hard, and then Carl and I left the restaurant. It was a sunny fall afternoon, and I insisted on a stroll along the Old Port, although by this time I was staggering. I leaned against my husband, who walked Tin Man stiff. We made our way toward the river. At the top of a steep cobblestone street, we came upon a blond man pushing an old lady in a wheelchair, a plaid blanket over her legs. The woman, who wore sunglasses and a rain bonnet, was so stooped, I figured she was snoozing. "Could you folks direct us to Chinatown?" the blond man asked. He was the strapping, milk-fed type, no older than twenty-five.

"Oh, I love Chinatown!" I slurred.

Carl gave directions, zigzagging his hand like an eel, while I stood there pretending to be sober. As the young man pointed toward Chinatown, his hand let go of the wheelchair, which slid forward and began zipping down the street.

I ran after the lady. "Stop! Stop!" I yelled. Halfway down the street, my heart hammering, I grabbed the back of the wheelchair, but then my ankle twisted and I fell to the ground. The wheelchair overturned and the sleeping lady pitched out and tumbled lifeless over the cobblestones.

"Peg!"

Carl came running toward me.

"The lady, the lady," I shouted. "Help the lady!"

She was lying still. Carl turned her over. Somehow her sunglasses and rain bonnet had stayed attached to her head. "What the hell?" Carl said. He picked the old lady up by the shoulders of her cardigan and shook her. Her head lolled. Her orthopedic shoes swung.

"Carl!"

"She's a dummy!" he yelled. He dropped the lady. He kicked her in the head.

The blond man was beside me, bending to help me up.

"Don't touch her," Carl hollered and lunged, swiping the guy with the back of his hand.

Out of nowhere came a bearded fellow with a handheld camera. He explained, meekly, barely looking at us, that we were the victims of a setup for the comedy festival, a candid-camera show called *Funny Weird or Funny Ha Ha?* He had a waiver for us to sign in his van parked across the street. I sat on the cobblestones, one knee scraped and bloody, my ankle throbbing, my husband kneeling beside me, a hand on my back. I was about to laugh till I turned to Carl. A vein in his neck looked as swollen as a garden hose. He stood, wrested the camera from the bearded guy and heaved it down the street. I expected sprockets and lenses to fly off, but the thing slid into the gutter intact.

"We'll sue," said Beard, warily.

"You fucking try," Carl snapped.

Beard took a cellphone from his pocket and flipped it open. Carl grabbed that too and flung it up on a balcony overlooking the street.

"You're crazy," Beard said and backed slowly away from my husband, who was a big, barrel-chested man.

"You hurt my wife," he yelled.

"Maybe she fell because she's had a tad too much to drink," Blond suggested. He leaned over me, his hands on his knees, and said, "Isn't that right, ma'am?"

Carl flew at him, tackling the young man. Beard ran up the street, shouting, "I'm calling the cops." I watched my sweet, docile husband, his fist full of blond hair, smash a man's face against cobblestones.

"Enough!" I yelled, panicked, stone-cold sober. "Carl, enough!"

He let go of the guy, who groaned and crawled away like a lizard, blood coursing from his nose. And my husband crawled toward me. On his hands and knees, his face warped, barely recognizable, he begged, "Enough."

After the gag with the cop in the garter belt, the camera zooms in on a cobblestone street. A snoozing woman in a wheelchair. The blond man, who eventually let the charges drop. I watch the people who signed the waiver, who ran after the dummy and didn't trip.

The crowd howls.

Every year, this screen shows the best of the sketches from years past. Our sketch is always among them.

The time Carl and I watched this screen together

we managed a nervous giggle. He said we should come back the next year and the year after that. Keep coming till we'd graduated to tears of laughter.

He died before we got that far.

I sit and watch the duped and the hoodwinked. I know these people well; I see them every year. The businessman who looks like Humpty Dumpty. The young Asian woman with purple streaks in her hair. The muscular bike courier who throws his bike down to chase after the dummy.

Carl and I, of course, never appear on screen. Still, I see us up there.

This year, with Wolf Blass prowling in my veins, the tears in my eyes aren't of laughter.

It's the last day of my vacation, and I'm dressing up. I have curled my hair and piled it atop my head. I'm wearing tomato red lipstick and contact lenses that turn my hazel eyes baby blue. My dress is gingham and cinched at the waist with a wide belt. High heels and a tight string of pearls complete the picture.

I'm Lucille Ball.

You zany redhead, says Carl from the bed.

I pick up the phone and call Max. I'm sending him a package by bus, I say.

"What is it?"

"Some of your stuff I don't have room for in my new place."

Max says that this morning he emailed me a digital picture of himself taken after his banana-peel accident. "With my two black eyes, I looked like a boxer. Really cool."

I tell him I don't have time to download his Fight Club membership card right now. "I'm heading off to AA."

"That again. You aren't sick of those meetings? You aren't ready to try something new?"

"New?" I say. "Like what? Crackheads Anonymous?"

"Too funny," he says in his bored-teenager tone.

I catch a glimpse of myself in the mirror: "Cross-dressers Anonymous?"

Max says, "Hardy har har."

From the bed we once shared, my dead husband suggests, *Necrophiliacs Anonymous?*

Before AA, I stop at the bus station. As I wait in line, I kiss my fingers with my Lucy lips and then stamp those red lips onto a box that once held a juice extractor.

"Safe journey."

In the basement of the Atwater Library, I'm standing in the women's washroom with Ricky Ricardo. His hair is greased back into a pompadour. He has on high-waisted slacks and a jacket with a handkerchief peeking out of his pocket.

"I'm nervous, Lucy." With his fake Latino accent, Tony the Greek says, "I don't have no acting 'sperience."

"That's bull," I say. "We alcoholics all have years of acting experience."

Wanda knocks on the washroom door, calling out, "Ready when you are." As Tony and I head into the meeting hall, everyone claps and whistles.

The story we're sharing tonight is that of Ricky and Lucy, sketches I've written and persuaded Tony to co-star in. Lucy hiding her Vitameatavegamin bottles in the clothes hamper. Ricky blowing a gasket. Lucy making her own wine by stomping barefoot in a vat of grapes. Ricky yelling in rapid-fire Spanish and calling Lucy a wino. Lucy wailing *Wahhhhhh!*

"Drink your way to health!" I shout and then roll my phony baby blues at my audience: Wanda, Andy, Marie-Ève, Stan, Huguette, Wendy, Michel, Ian and the others. Whenever these people stand up at the front and share their stories, a hush falls over the room, a stillness that feels sacred. I love that stillness. It keeps me coming back here. But tonight it's not what I want. Tonight I want this room ringing with laughter.

EXTREMITIES

THE GLOVES ADORED the sensation. Fingers sliding through their cashmere lining, diverging in ten directions, butting against their innermost tips. A sated, exquisite feeling. Heavenly.

The hands trembled. The gloves trembled. Deep inside them, ten fingerprint swirls lit up like the elements of a stove. The juices of the hands, minute droplets of perspiration and skin oils, trickled into the cashmere and were absorbed into the supple, pale pink calfskin of which the gloves were made. This fluid carried with it the secrets of the hands—more secrets than could be revealed by random lines etched on a palm. Instantly the gloves learned the identity of the woman whose hands were the first to burrow inside them. Her name was Dagmar Zavichak. The gloves' first love.

Not one goddamn scratch on me. You try falling fifty thousand fucking feet to the ground and see how you look. Granted, I landed in a rose bush. But, still, roses have thorns, and I'm scratch-free, baby. Nails clipped and buffed, cuticles tidied, skin smelling of that mint moisturizer slathered on last night. I'm a big foot, man. Size twelve American! I've got little blond hairs on the knuckles of my toes. Blond as the hair on a baby's head—not those rat-ugly black hairs some guys got growing out of their feet. I got me some pumiced heels. I got me some delicate ankles. No shit, I'm size twelve, and I've got the ankles of a ballerina. Ha! I'm tripping out. I'm flying. I'm doing the fucking cancan, man. It's like I'm on speed. Ironic that, because what I don't got, above those delicate ankles of mine, is Captain Robert "Speed" Spedoski.

The calfskin gloves, perched on a pair of mannequin hands atop a glass display case, enjoyed observing their beloved at work. For the past ten years, Dagmar Zavichak had been employed as a loss-prevention agent—which is to say a store detective—at Winston's, an upscale department store in downtown Chicago. It was her professional duty to appear as inconspicuous as possible, no more substantial, really, than the tissue paper wrapped by a salesclerk around a newly purchased sweater. The gloves believed she rose stupendously to this challenge. To salesclerks who inquired about her unconventional career, she would profess, "I must appear vaporous, a sort of floater in other people's eyes."

To this end, she did not dress in the more ostentatious designer clothing popular in the store, instead favouring Winston's own rather conservative label, Clémence, on which she received a twenty percent discount. In fact, in her decade of employment at Winston's, every item of clothing she had bought there bore the Clémence label. Needless to say, this loyalty to one label worried the gloves, as they were sewn in an Italian house of design known as Giuseppe La Leggia. Yet the gloves were consoled by the fact that each day, as Dagmar Zavichak wandered the store shadowing potential "perps"—the term that loss-prevention agents applied to shoplifters—she would always linger in leather goods and succumb to the urge to try the gloves on.

In calfskin, her hands could move in ways they had never done before. They could make a deft point, beckon gracefully. Gesticulate. In calfskin, they became as dexterous as the hands of baseball umpires, traffic cops and the deaf. In calfskin, her hands radiated possibility.

Speed's idol, Neil Armstrong, was named after an appendage, an arm, but it was his right foot—have I mentioned I'm a rightie?—that made that one small step that turned into a giant leap. Our man Speed, ever since he was an eleven-year-old, one gimlet eye trained on a telescope, had dreamed of being the first to set foot on a blood-red world named after the Roman god of war—Mars. But unless Mars has rose bushes, an above-ground pool, a split-level bungalow, a barbecue grill and a banquet table, you can bet Speed's right nut he never made it.

On Mars, Speed would've weighed a paltry sixty-nine pounds. His day would've lasted forty minutes longer than on Earth. At the equator, he could've basked in a midday temp of seventy degrees Fahrenheit. He would've seen gullies, broad plains, mountains higher than Everest, swirling winds called dust devils that whip the soil into red tornadoes. He would've seen two moons in the sky, so tiny he could've jogged around those buggers in an afternoon. I could blab on about Mars, but none of this tells you much about Speed, other than that his lifelong dream was to make a forty-million-mile leap.

That leap was never *my* dream. My name, by the way, is Larry. I have no last name. But if I did, I'd want a hero's name like Neil Strongarm. Hey, hey, I know, call me Larry Footloose. Ha! My lifelong dream: to be free of Speed.

Mission accomplished.

The gloves looked forward to Mondays, Wednesdays, Fridays and Sundays, as these were the days Dagmar Zavichak worked at Winston's. On Wednesdays, they became positively giddy with anticipation because between one and two o'clock, her lunch hour, the gloves accompanied the loss-prevention agent into the real world. Why Wednesdays? Because that was the rule. On Wednesdays, Dagmar Zavichak slipped the gloves from the mannequin hands and into her Clémence jacket, deft as the nimblest pickpocket.

The ride in the loss-prevention agent's pocket, as she drifted through women's wear, down the escalator, around endless cosmetic counters and out the revolving front door, was the part of the day's journey the gloves least enjoyed, for they usually shared that dark, intimate pouch with a pair of balled-up mittens whose damp wool and graceless shape the calfskin gloves found particularly disheartening. But today the mittens were not there. The gloves had the roomy pocket to themselves. As their beloved scurried away from Winston's, they fell one against the other in what might be deemed their first attempt at applause.

What went wrong? What happened to the *Zoë X*? Probably something unfathomably stupid brought the bugger down. Remember the *Challenger* back in '86? Disintegrated a minute after liftoff. Remember the news clips, the horror-struck spectators squinting up at the sky? And that high-school teacher, Christa McAuliffe! Oh God in heaven, she was my type, that Christa was, with those honest brown eyes, that naturally curly hair. Smart. Good with kids. That tight blue spacesuit zipped halfway down her chest! Not Speed's type, but mine.

Anyway, the *Challenger* rode into the sky on the back of a huge blimp-shaped fuel tank, like a remora on a shark. Also attached to that tank were two rocket boosters to provide thrust. The joints of those boosters were sealed with what you call O-rings. Picture the rubber washers in your faucet, only bigger. Well, it was thirty-two degrees Fahrenheit the morning of the *Challenger* launch, and so the rubber O-rings were too cold to expand and seal the joints. Hot gases and flames shot out of the booster, causing the whole kit-and-caboodle to blow. Where's the justice, man: Christa was done in by a fucking washer.

How thrillingly loud was the world outside Winston's easy-listening cocoon. Hare Krishnas shook tambourines. A skateboarder cursed at a taxi. Pedestrians shouted into cellphones. An ambulance dopplered by. After indolent days atop their display case, the gloves were elated to be on the move, to be filled with hands whose fingertips exuded the pungent smell of aged cheddar from the sandwich Dagmar Zavichak had hastily eaten before fetching the gloves.

Where would their beloved take them today? In their outings thus far, the gloves had travelled to the Art Institute of Chicago, a bookshop and a supermarket, and each time they learned something new about the loss-prevention agent, something alluding to a pattern as persistent as the black-eyed Susans running the length of her silk scarf. At the art museum, they learned that her favourite artist was Paul Klee, for she looked only at his paintings, not once glancing sideways to view, say, a Kandinsky. At the bookshop, she riffled only through the works of the novelist John Irving. At the supermarket, the gloves handled prickly pears and a pineapple. What bliss! But any canned or boxed food they placed in her basket sported the exact same label, so that at the checkout counter the cashier exclaimed, "You sure like Consumer's Choice!" Dagmar Zavichak, the gloves' beloved, replied, "I'm a very loyal shopper."

So you want to hear about Speed. Everybody always wants the nitty-gritty on Robert Spedoski. Now that he's the new Icarus, they'll no doubt want even more. You want to hear why he and I didn't see eye to eye. To put it simply: Speed wasn't up to snuff. Speed didn't have *The Right Snuff.* Ha! You hear about transsexuals being born in the wrong bodies. Men who don't want their pricks. Well, I was born in the wrong body, too. He was a prick and I didn't want him.

No, but maybe I'm being too hard on Speed. Give the guy a break, Larry. Cut him some slack. He treated you okay. For crying out loud, he massaged your tootsies with mint moisturizer he forked out twenty bucks for. Where would you be without him? I'll tell you where: right here, in a rose bush in a suburban backyard where some bald dude in a suit is carrying a bowl of fruit punch across his lawn.

One calfskin glove gripped the man's hand and released. As it did so, the man's lifeline and other traces of his touch faded from the glove's palm like a child's drawings in the sand, washed away by the surf. The gloves could not know this man the way they knew Dagmar Zavichak. She was their beloved; he was merely a fleeting encounter in a coffee shop.

For this outing, this blind date, the gloves enjoyed a perfect view of the proceedings: they sat decorously on the table, ten digits entwined. They glowed pink and throbbed like a calf's excised heart. "The usual?" asked the waitress. Their beloved answered, "Naturally." For his part, the man requested orange pekoe tea, and the gloves knew that Dagmar Zavichak admired how he delivered his order forcefully, as if no other tea leaf would do. This outing looked promising at first. But later, as the man talked about himself and the mutual funds he sold, he spilled three drops of his orange pekoe and neglected to mop them up, he scattered granules of sugar on his placemat and inadvertently crunched them with his elbows, and, for no apparent reason, he inserted a finger into his ear and shook the digit vigorously. Such behaviour would not do.

Consequently, Dagmar Zavichak grew restless, as did the gloves. They fidgeted. They tucked a lock of hair behind her ear. They plucked a loose eyelash from her cheek. They raised her bowl of café au lait to her lips so she could gulp the warm froth. Soon, one glove was leaping in front of her face to expose the wristwatch just below its cuff. "Time flies," their beloved said. The date freeze-dried a smile. He was not, the gloves knew, Mr. Klee or Mr. Irving. There were so many ways a man could fail, and this man had.

Okay, this is going back five years. NASA has announced how many greenbacks Speed's jaunt to the red planet is gonna gobble up, and he's miffed because the media is moaning that the money should go to a more worthy cause. Channel it into Fruit Loops so no American kiddie goes to school with a gurgling tummy. Funnel it into defence against those godless nations beheading our citizens live on the Web. Still, people love Speed, and NASA knows it. He can run a five-minute mile. He's got a black belt in karate. He's eloquent. Just listen to him talk to an auditorium full of students at Carnegie Mellon University. He likens the *Zoë X* mission to a certain journey launched in 1492 by Mr. Cristoforo Colombo. Each young man in the room is King Ferdinand, each young woman Queen Isabella. And they're buying what he's selling, namely that finding primitive, methane-farting microbes far beneath the Martian surface is vital to their VIP-DVD-SUV existences on Earth. Speed explains that life sprouted on the young

Mars and may still linger underground. "Life tries to hang on," he tells the students. "Life does everything it can to survive."

Later, walking to his hotel, he cuts through an alleyway, and there's this pie-eyed bum sitting on a smashed microwave oven, some down-and-out who smells like a bag of rotting onions. The bum scrambles up, blocks Speed's path, throws him a goofy smile. In Speed's head, an editorial hollers: *Funnel the money into housing for the homeless!* "Spare some—" the bum gets out before Speed's right foot—old Larry himself, dressed in a leather brogue—connects with the guy's mouth. The bum pitches backwards and crashes down. Blood dribbles from his split lip. Is he dead? Speed stands over him. No, he's still breathing. Speed says, "Sometimes life hangs on too long."

Of course, Dagmar Zavichak was not the only woman to slip her hands deep into the calfskin gloves. Yet no other woman lingered inside them; no other handprints burned into their skin. Stuffed with the lardy hands of these other women, the gloves felt like a trollop; filled with Dagmar Zavichak's slender hands, they felt like a pampered mistress dined at a fashionable restaurant while the wife, the pair of oblivious wool mittens, remained sequestered at home. For the gloves' next outing, Dagmar Zavichak took them to lunch at Chez Julien, where they fingered satisfyingly heavy silverware and a linen napkin still warm from the dryer.

As a special surprise, she ordered the veal cutlet and kept her hands gloved throughout her meal. She pricked the morsels of meat with her fork, brought them to her lips and slowly chewed the dead calf. As she swallowed, the calfskin gloves quivered, for now they were, in a way, inside of her, just as she was inside of them.

Yet when the meal came to an end, their beloved returned them once again to their post on the display case at Winston's. How they yearned to be hers alone. Would their beloved ever take them home? They dreamed of this home, this mittenless home with prints by Mr. Klee on the walls, novels by Mr. Irving on the bookshelves, Consumer's Choice canned goods in the cupboards. Beneath the quiet equanimity, the simmering obsessions.

My cover's blown! Mr. Suburbia, the bald dude in the suit, is squatting in front of my rose bush, and two guesses who he comes face to foot with. Well, he freaks. His face contorts like a cartoon: eyes bugging, mouth gaping, nostrils flared. He grunts, falls backwards, drops his clippers and the roses he's cut. I'm thinking he's having a fucking heart attack—he's a pudgy older dude, a bit jowly, grey beard—but no, he springs back up and moves in close, parting the leaves of the bush with his hands. "Jesus H. Christ," he mutters. Then the guy starts combing the backyard, foraging through the hedges, peering into the swimming pool. He's looking for other parts! What does he expect to find? A kneecap behind the compost bin, an elbow on the roof of the shed, Speed's right nut under the barbecue? It's like he's Isis, the Egyptian goddess, looking for pieces of her dismembered husband, Osiris. That's a good one: our golden boy, Robert Spedoski, as god of the underworld.

They were the first male hands to penetrate the gloves. Small and moist, they slid in easily. As ten fingers flexed like boys in gym class doing deep knee bends, ten fingerprints burned into the gloves' tips; if the calfskin still had hair, that hair would have been bristling. These hands were jumpy, kinetic, and the perspiration seeping into the cashmere lining could have curdled milk. At the other end of the appendages was a man whose thin moustache appeared pencilled on. His eyes had bulbous whites and pinprick pupils. The gloves recalled a watercolour at the art museum; *Face in Hand* was the painting, a self-portrait of Mr. Klee resting his head in his palm. Yet this man was not gentle Mr. Klee. This man, the gloves realized, was a bandit. This man was a perp.

A wedding reception, man. A goddamn wedding reception. People mill around the yard, schmooze and guffaw. Wine glasses tinkle. Little kids weave in and out of everybody's legs in a squealing game of tag. People wolf down calzones brought in from the restaurant owned by the father of the bride, pudgy Mr. Suburbia. Minutes after he discovered yours truly, his guests started swarming into his backyard. He barely had time to drag the barbecue in front of my rose bush. But I can see under the belly of the thing. Larry's got a good view.

Guess what. Fuck me if one of the guests isn't a dead ringer for the dead astronautess Christa McAuliffe. Same honest face, same curly hair. Dressed in pale pink, she is—dress, shoes and gloves. She and the bride are standing away from the crowd, not far from my bush, and Christa is talking about Speed. "So close to his dream he could almost lick the ice crystals on Mars," she says. "Imagine spending every breath of your life longing for something you'll never have." Her voice sounds sad. Don't be sad,

Christa. The lanky bride, in her silver sheath of a dress, looks like a rocket booster. She says Christa is being a gloomy Gus on her special day. She says she's got her dream: the giddy groom doing cartwheels under the clothesline to entertain the kiddies. Then the father of the bride butts in. "Come away from there," he says, glancing at my rose bush. "Come join the living."

Soon everybody's dancing. Man, I'd like to trip the light fantastic myself. A cancan, man, but no can do. My dream's come true, but without Speed, I ain't the twinkletoes I used to be.

While the perp stood at the urinal, the calfskin gloves, appalled and frightened by the turn of events, attempted to lose themselves in memories of happier times. As the stinking stream of urine sizzled against porcelain, the gloves drifted back to their childhood in a factory in Florence. The good, heady smell of leather. The lilting voices of sewing machines in song. The needle gently puncturing the skin. Gloves in a spectrum of colours lying together like litters of kittens. Each finger on each glove one possible direction in which their life might point them.

The calfskin gloves had not dreamed that this would be their fate: shaking the last dribbly drops out of a thick, dim-witted digit devoid of nail, knuckle, fingerprint. The gloves shoved this flesh back into the perp's pants, raised his zipper and, in front of the restroom mirror, combed themselves through his hair. They shuddered at the sight of his face, as milky white as cooked veal. Away from the mirror, they pushed open the door and there, standing in the little hallway, was their saviour. Beloved! Oh, such sweet, sweet relief.

"Sir, we do not allow customers to bring merchandise into the restrooms." Her voice wavered. "Oh, so sorry," said the perp. One gloved thumb pressed the button on a drinking fountain as the perp bent over and slurped. When he stood, Dagmar Zavichak was still there. "May I have the gloves?" she said, her voice more forceful. "Yes, yes, of course," he said. But the perp hesitated. The gloves tensed. Then his arms shot up and the gloves grabbed their beloved by the neck.

I haven't mentioned Marty, have I? Marty was my partner. Marty was a leftie, and like most lefties he was a bit slow on the uptake. But loyal. God, Marty was as loyal as a golden goddamn retriever. You want proof? His name was originally Lionel, but he changed it to Marty when Speed started obsessing over the red planet. I said to him, "Why not Marsy?" And he said, "Oh, Larry, Marsy ain't a name."

Still, Marty was a good guy. He'd scratch my back, I'd scratch his. But he never really understood Speed. Not like I did. For instance, not one family dinner went by when Speed didn't curse his dad, badmouth his mom and toot his own horn to his brothers, but Marty would make excuses. "It ain't easy being a hero to the nation, Larry," he'd say. Or he'd change the topic: "Remember when Speed was eleven and took us roller-skating for the first time? Remember how clumsy we all were? Even you were laughing, Larry. Even stick-in-the-mud you. You said it was like trying to walk on the frigging moon, excuse my French."

Marty was a nostalgic bugger. Poor good-natured Marty. Wonder if he felt it. Felt what I did as the *Zoë X* lifted its gargantuan ass off the tarmac and blasted toward the heavens. Speed never shared much with me and Marty. We were too far from his brain, too far from his heart. But in those final moments, I felt something course through his veins, something as clean and fortifying as milk. A mix of resignation and serenity.

That's when I knew.

I knew what Speed had already realized: that the *Zoë X* would blow. He knew there were hiccups in its design, something obviously harder to fix than an idiotic O-ring, but he never pointed out the glitches for fear of having the project shelved for good. Speed couldn't wait any longer. All his life he'd wanted to be millions of miles away from the rest of mankind. He couldn't wait a fucking day longer. "Goodbye, Marty," I said as the cabin disintegrated.

The gloves had never been closer to their beloved. Dagmar Zavichak had sunk her flesh into them, but never had they sunk their flesh into her. Through the strings of muscle in her neck, the buttery-soft gloves could feel her heart beating, beating, beating, pounding, pounding. From her mouth came the bleating of a caged, motherless calf. Her bare hands tried prying the gloves from her neck, but the gloves were reluctant to break their warm embrace. Up to the perp's face, her hands rose. They scratched his cheeks. They poked his eyes. Only then did the calfskin gloves release their grip.

Oh, but what had they done? What had the gloves done? The shame! The pink of their leather surely deepened from such grievous shame. Yet the gloves had no chance to apologize to their beloved, now slumped against the wall, her hands fluttering at her throat, because the perp scuttled off and then broke into a run, his arms pumping, the gloves slapping past racks of clothing, knocking a wide-brimmed flying saucer of a hat off a woman's head. Out the revolving door they pushed, their lining drenched from the perp's spongy palms.

In the spring morning, a tribe of Hare Krishnas waved their tambourines. The perp jounced their robes as he shot by, pulling at the calfskin as if it were scorching his hands. He peeled the gloves off and, frantic, pushed them through the swinging lid of a streetside recycling bin, where they landed crumpled atop a heap of soda cans tacky from spilt orangeade.

Lying there in the dark, their cuffs turned inside out, they told themselves they deserved this fate. They had betrayed their beloved. They had grown so attached to Dagmar Zavichak that they had wanted to be permanently attached to her. Like an appendage. Like a hand. Like that hand now snaking through the lid of the recycling bin, its familiar Y-shaped lifeline a divining rod. "Here we are!" the gloves called out. "Oh, sweet Jesus, here we are!"

The party's over. It's midnight and everybody's moseyed on home. Around me, I hear crickets playing a concert with their wings as violins. A neighbour's revolving sprinkler whizzes and tweets. Tonight the sky's cloudless. Look due south fifty degrees above the horizon and you'll spot a red star. Guess who?

The door at the back of the house clacks open. The porch light clicks on. Two figures walk across the yard, one holding a flashlight whose beam homes in on a yard swing. "I'm sure my gloves are here somewhere, Mr. DiMaria," a voice says. A voice I recognize from the party. The voice of Christa McAuliffe. "Oh, sweet Jesus," I call out. "I'm over here!"

Snug inside her pocket, the gloves could hear Dagmar Zavichak's co-workers cooing with concern. "Your throat," one woman said, "will surely bruise." "The police," one man said, "must be called in." "He got away," their beloved repeated. "He got away with a pair of calfskin gloves!" "Such mayhem over a pair of gloves," said another man. "Oh, but they're lost," their beloved exclaimed. "They're gone!"

Inside her pocket, the gloves were happy: they were going home.

It's two a.m. For light, we've got a big communion wafer of a moon and a flashlight lying on the ground not far from my bush. Mr. Suburbia—Mr. DiMaria— is over by the shed, where he's been shovelling for the past fifteen minutes. His backyard is where Speed took his final step for man, and Mr. DiMaria doesn't want that kind of notoriety. After digging his hole, he leans his shovel against the shed, wipes his brow and picks up a cardboard box. As he comes for me, I rec-ognize the box for what it is. A shoebox. Fitting.

He sets it down and scoots the barbecue aside. From the barbecue hang what look like hot dog tongs. He uses them. He parts the leaves and branches, and those god-damn metal claws drag me out by the toes. He drops me into the box, muttering, "I'm sorry, Speed." I want to say, *The name's Larry,* but instead I think the same thing: I'm sorry, Speed. Sorry that in the days counting down to your big countdown I kept hoping you'd fail big time.

The gloves' presence in their beloved's home had ramifications. A ripple effect. Out with the old—out with Mr. Klee, Mr. Irving, the Clémence clothing, the Consumer's Choice—and in with the new. New outfits to be hung in the closet, a new artist to be selected for the walls, new novels to be read, new food to be sampled. Such a hullabaloo that their beloved grew cranky and eventually quite ill.

One day, after a sobbing breakdown during which she tore to bits her new Roy Lichtenstein poster, *Study of Hands,* Dagmar Zavichak changed everything back. The old—the familiar, soothing old—returned. Oh, hello again, Mr. Irving and Mr. Klee. Welcome home! As for the calfskin gloves, they were thrust into the farthest reaches of her closet. There they waited, fearful of their own waning love. There were so many ways a pair of gloves could fail, and these gloves had, hadn't they? Yet they remained hopeful, knowing that one day they would again be brought out into the world. At Winston's, their outings were restricted to Wednesdays. Why Wednesdays? Because that was the rule. In Dagmar Zavichak's home, the new rule was this: she could wear her pink gloves exclusively to events out of state. For instance, the wedding of her friend Theresa down in Florida.

Mr. DiMaria retrieves his flashlight and bends over the shoebox to examine me up close. My gorgeousness. But he goes wobbly-kneed and bumps against the barbecue—and down flutter two wings, two pink angels that alight on my hide. The gloves Christa had come back for and never found. "If I find them, I'll mail them to you," Mr. DiMaria had promised. "They're nothing special," Christa had replied. "Give them to charity." And he will. He'll give them to me, a guy with one foot in the grave. Christa's hands to caress me, tickle my sole. Hands to hold me forever. What a gift, man. Like they say about donated organs: the gift of a lifetime.

———

On a wedding day in Florida, the gloves tasted the fluids of Dagmar Zavichak's body. In a hotel room, they pasted a pincurl to her forehead with the saliva from her mouth. In a church, they rubbed away tears as the priest declared "till death do you part." In a parking lot, they wiped her runny nose as the Florida flora coughed up its pollen. In a bathroom at the father of the bride's home, they slid a tissue between her legs and absorbed a drop of urine. Yet these fluids carried no secrets. Urine, mucous, saliva, tears, sweat—they were no more evocative than the flat ginger ale Dagmar Zavichak was sipping at the backyard reception. As she sliced herself some wedding cake, the gloves half-hoped she would plunge the knife into her wrist. Blood! Perhaps only blood could rekindle the love, the extreme love, that she and the gloves had once shared.

It came as no surprise to the gloves when Dagmar Zavichak mislaid them atop a barbecue grill. From their perch, they watched the celebrations, the hot sun bleaching their skin. They studied the people gathered there. Among these guests was perhaps a new beloved, for earlier in the day, as Theresa Fritz, née DiMaria, squealed on the church steps, the gloves had leapt into the air to pluck the bouquet of flowers from the sky.

———

On their cardboard roof comes the pitter-patter not of rain but of earth. Falling earth. In their bed, they intertwine. Beloved and beloved and beloved. Fingers stroke. Toes wriggle. A heel grinds. The sole sweats on a palm. A glove stretches open its calfskin cuff, and the foot thrusts in, the toe print of the big toe as enormous and electrifying as a whirlpool galaxy. Their love is obsessive. Yet they take their time. There is no rush: they have the rest of their lives. They are brides and groom, and this is their wedding night.

JAYBIRD

ACT I: THE SEDUCTION

THE LAID-BACK LOOK WAS A LIE. His mussed-up hair came courtesy of a mud putty that had set him back twelve bucks. That weathered jean shirt with the missing pocket, well, he'd combed the second-hand shops for that. A shirt that lied that he didn't spend time thinking about shirts.

Benoit Doré glimpsed his face in the mirrored wall behind the bar. Cocked an eyebrow just to see his reflection do likewise. Then he paid for his Perrier and wedged the lemon slice through the bottle neck. Mineral water. It didn't square with his image as a doleful brooder. Except it did if you'd read that profile on him last week in Montreal's *Voir* magazine. To up his angst, he'd hinted at a struggle with alcohol. Such a crock. Boxes of herbal teas tumbled out of his kitchen cupboards.

Before his stage debut, he'd worked at this same bar. It was in the lobby of the Confiserie, a sleek theatre with polished metal surfaces and walls painted a streaky, blood-clot red. The space once housed a candy factory and was haunted, so people joked, by the ghosts of gummi bears past. Benoit glanced around the place. Some big names were there that night. Much bigger than his.

He made the rounds. Shook hands with old, surly Georges Valiquette, whose breath reeked of Scotch and whose cauliflower knob of a nose Benoit found both repulsive and oddly fascinating. Pascale Chastenay came over to them, blew smoke in their faces from her stogie and then griped about a review in *Le Devoir* that claimed she had a reptilian presence onstage. "Do I look like a toad to you?" She did, but Benoit simply said, "Toads are amphibians." He excused himself and waved hello to Cécile

Bellehumeur, who was sitting broomstick straight, humourless as ever, as she argued politics with Luc Bourguignon, who jiggled his knee like an epileptic and crunched through a bag of sour cream and onion chips, the crumbs falling like dandruff flakes down his black turtleneck.

Dany Savard motioned Benoit over. He sat with a beautiful woman at a tiny table whose metal top looked like a pizza pan. "Meet Mélanie, my mentee," Dany said. Benoit said hi and glanced at Mélanie's smooth, tanned legs. Dany threw Benoit a smirk that said, *Man did I luck out.*

For its tenth anniversary, the Confiserie's artistic director had recruited ten alumni for a mentorship program called Mentorat. The ten actors (the mentors) would each work with an apprentice (the mentees) on a ten-minute sketch to be staged in ten days' time. Tonight was the first introductory meeting, and the actors and apprentices milled around the lobby, chatting together.

Off the lobby, in the hall leading to the theatre, were framed photographs of the actors in action. Luc Bourguignon hamming it up in *L'amour-propre de M. Snead.* Dany Savard and Lucie Faucher at loggerheads in *Notre maison n'est pas encore habitable.* Cécile Bellehumeur's body lying lifeless onstage in *Corps du délit.* Pascale Chastenay licking out the innards of a papaya in *À des fins pacifiques.*

Benoit's apprentice—her name was Madeleine—was standing in that hall. "Here's one of you," she said as Benoit approached. "Jesus, honey, you look creepy scowling like that."

In the photo, Benoit scratched his head with the butt of a gun and clutched a scruffy teddy bear. His eyes were glaring and ringed in kohl.

"That's from *Achale-moi pus.* I played a crack dealer."

"I saw you in that. You were horrible."

"Horrible?"

"I mean your character. What a psycho. You do psycho good. That's why I asked to be paired with you."

She had requested him. He liked that.

Madeleine was a few years older than Benoit, probably mid-thirties. She was plump and had small, deep-set eyes and a J-shaped scar, like a fish hook, that dropped from one nostril to her top lip. He'd met her briefly a couple of times before because she worked for Agence Wingood, the talent agency that had just signed him. Her job was to look after the actors' schedules and direct them to shoots and auditions. You wanted to know where you had to be, what time, with whom, you called Madeleine.

"I guess you applied for Mentorat to see what we rats really do," Benoit said.

Hysterical laughter erupted in the lobby. Someone was actually yodelling. Probably his friend Dany, the nut.

"I wanna be a rat, too." Madeleine's face suddenly turned mischievous and conspiratorial. "At least, for ten minutes." She glanced at the picture on the wall, and her smiling face reflected in Benoit's photographed scowl like the masks of comedy and tragedy.

"Jeez, what a creep," she said.

Benoit sipped his Perrier and stared at his scowl.

"Well, I'm not really a creep," he finally said, although most of the time he felt like one. "You should know from the get-go, Madeleine, that acting is lying. Can you lie?"

He doubted it.

"I can try."

The first woman Benoit remembered seducing was in his parents' health food store. At the time, he'd been a six-year-old with a tangle of dark hair and eyes the colour of the sky-blue crayon. He sat on a stool near the cash register, nibbling a square of chalky carob. If he flashed a cockeyed smile, he knew the woman paying for her pine nuts would smile back at him.

He smiled. She smiled. She ruffled his hair and said, "That smile deserves a tip."

She left him her change—seventy-five cents.

I can make money at this, he thought.

Once the woman had gone, his mother called to his father, who was stocking cans of beans. "Ronald, our son's a gigolo!"

An updated version of that goofy smile was still in his repertoire of facial expressions, along with a cocked and inquisitive eyebrow, a smug smirk, a hateful sneer, a lascivious leer, a puzzled stare and his trademark, an arresting glare through dark bangs. Then there were his bodily gestures, his noncommittal shrug, his fervent nod, his lethargic slouch and so on.

He lived in a third-floor loft owned by an aunt, who supported the arts, she claimed, by not charging him rent. His furniture consisted mostly of an over-stuffed sofa, bookcases and a bed around which he could pull a dark velvet curtain that hung from the ceiling. Five ficus plants, each a different species, grew from hefty terra cotta pots, one so tall its leaves touched the ceiling. In one corner, he had put together a makeshift stage where he'd rehearse his lines and hone his skills, often watching himself in front of the wood-framed mirror that hung there. He also had a video camera set atop a tripod to tape himself.

When he wasn't practising at home, when he was, say, ordering takeout, riding the subway, listening to his mother's monologues, training on the rowing machine, washing his armpits, playing pool with Dany, making love to Julie or Sophie or Hélène or any of the other women he seduced, he was still acting. A director out to butter him up once called him a natural. But he wasn't. He knew that. He worked to appear natural. Constantly. While ordering banh pho bo at Pho Viet, he might practise sounding impatient or meek or befuddled or gleeful. Clutching his warm takeout bag, he'd walk home, thinking, How'd I do? And a voice would rebuke him: Man, you're as limp as a rice noodle.

"Jaybird?"

"Yes, jaybird."

"What exactly is a jaybird?"

"Good question," Madeleine said. "You know, I'm not too sure, but I imagine a jaybird is any type of jay. Like the blue jay, of course, but I think there are grey jays and, oh gosh, maybe brown jays, too."

Benoit and Madeleine sat centre stage at the Confiserie. The lights reflected off her hair, which was the blondish colour of construction boots. Beside her were the two items she'd arrived with: a hat box patterned with white roses, and a chunky boom box, the kind rappers blasted. She unclasped her hat box and drew out a white Duo-Tang folder. Stencilled on the cover was the word JAYBIRD.

"My title doesn't actually refer to the bird."

Madeleine had written her own sketch. It was bound to be amateurish, cringe-worthy. How would Benoit dissuade her? He'd brought along a few potential scripts from home. In his favourite, a despondent cabdriver made amends to a woman whose son he had run over.

"I've heard you're an actor who takes chances. Do you?" Her small eyes looked fervid.

"Sure, I do."

"Good, because I'm giving you a chance to take." She handed him the Duo-Tang. He flipped through. There were three pages, a different title typed on each:

ACT I: THE SEDUCTION

ACT II: THE HUMILIATION

ACT III: THE FANTASY

"All righty, let's get started." She stood and rubbed her hands together. "In Act I, you stand at the front, your back to the audience." She walked downstage and then faced him. She was dressed in thin-ribbed corduroys and a paisley blouse. "You're naked."

He cocked his eyebrow.

"Don't get all bent out of shape. I'll be naked, too."

He glanced into the wings to see if anybody was listening. Nobody was around.

"The stage is pitch-black, except for a spotlight illuminating your, um, buttocks."

In his lap, under ACT I: THE SEDUCTION, he read, *Two mounds of fat, skin and muscle dance a duet.*

"Your buttocks gyrate, wiggle, clench their muscles. Your butt gives the performance of its life."

He barked a laugh.

She gave him a thin smile. "The audience might think it's a joke at first, but soon they'll see the beauty of your ass."

He held the script over his lap as if to hide his dick. He already felt naked in front of this woman who for weeks had been nothing more than a pleasant phone voice ensuring that he'd arrive on time for his audition for a frozen-waffle commercial.

"When your solo ends, the lights come up and I walk on in the buff."

He turned to page 2, ACT II: THE HUMILIATION, as Madeleine set the scene. "You get out a Magic Marker." She went to her hat box and withdrew a blue felt-tip pen. "You become a kind of deranged plastic surgeon. You dot lines across my body where excess fat needs trimming. I need to be sleek, streamlined, balanced, you say. You want to siphon out some fat and inject it into my boobs."

From her hat box, she took out a rubber Halloween mask. A red bow crammed into a black pincushion of hair. Eyes like charcoal briquettes. It was the little girl from the Nancy comics. "My face is making the audience uncomfortable, you say, and so you slip this mask over my head."

She put the mask on, and Benoit felt a mix of queasiness and adrenaline. The mask muffled her voice. "I've suggested a whole bunch of lines for you in the script, but feel free to improvise. Be brutal. The crueller, the better."

He looked down at the script. Words jumped out: *You chinless wonder, you homely half-wit.* Then a line: *That unused purse you couldn't give away at your garage sale, well, that was your pussy.*

Extreme. This woman was not what he'd expected. Did he like that? He wasn't sure. He felt uneasy. He pictured the stun-gunned look on the faces of Georges Valiquette, Cécile Bellehumeur and the other mentors. "Man, we'd have the audience squirming," he muttered.

"Honey, they won't be able to squirm," the Nancy mask replied. "They'll be riveted to their seats." She bent and pushed a button on her black boom box. A cassette began playing. Strings and brass. Classical music. "The prologue from Tchaikovsky's *La belle au bois dormant*," she said, and Benoit nodded, pretending to recognize the piece.

"Act III begins. My solo."

He turned to the last page of the script. Under ACT III: THE FANTASY were two words: "*Scène dansante.*"

She flung off her Nancy mask. Kicked off her loafers. Unbuttoned her blouse. Yanked down her trousers. She stood there in beige panties and a beige bra. She had sweet sloping shoulders, a bit of a paunch, small breasts, wide thighs. Her skin looked white and cool like bathtub enamel. He expected her to take off her bra, but she didn't. He sat stock-still, transfixed. She stood on tiptoes, hands poised over her head, fingertips touching. Her dance began. Her hands extended gracefully. She bent into a plié, straightened and then skipped across the stage. She pirouetted, whirled, spun. She balanced on one leg, swung her arms higher and higher. Her dance was not modern. It wasn't the experimental dance—twitching, stamping, spastic—he was used to seeing, but rather the kind of dance with willowy ballerinas and tutus. Except Madeleine was not willowy. She had no tutu. Her flesh was her tutu. She laid her body on the stage and swished her legs through the air. Dainty kicks.

Her head lolled from side to side. As the strings faded out, she sat up and smiled. A beaming, beatific smile.

He smiled back and clapped. She was actually a very decent dancer. Still, he couldn't agree to this. Too dicey. He'd somehow sweet-talk her into his sketch about the remorseful cabbie.

She clambered up and hopped clumsily into her clothes. "I picked you, Benoit," she said, buttoning her blouse, "because those other actors all pretend they're experimental, but what makes them really salivate is a starring role in a comfy sitcom."

He laughed and nodded.

"But you, sir, are intrepid," she said. "You've got balls."

The expression came to him: Naked as a jaybird.

But then he thought, Jays are covered in feathers. They aren't naked.

Dany Savard's apprentice wanted to play Laura in *La ménagerie de verre.* "Mélanie's got this whole victim fantasy. Wants to limp across the stage with a broken unicorn," Dany said as he sank the six ball. *Voir* magazine had recently called Dany seductively handsome. But to Benoit, his friend's face looked out of kilter, like somebody had sawn it in half vertically and glued it back together.

Dany chalked his pool cue. "She's got freckles down her cleavage. Think I can get her to stroke my unicorn horn?"

"Don't be a letch," Benoit said. "Besides, Jasmine would skin you." Jasmine was Dany's girlfriend.

"Hand jobs aren't cheating, Ben," Dany said. "It's in the Civil Code."

"Which section?"

"224."

"Paragraph?"

"Eight."

Benoit laughed and tried to forget that a year ago he'd slept with Jasmine. Dany didn't know this. He'd been off in Yellowknife, shooting a movie. At the time, Jasmine told Benoit that Dany was suffering from "erectile dysfunction triggered by performance anxiety" and if she and Benoit screwed around, maybe she could tough it out with Dany till he straightened out his act. To quell his guilt, Benoit pretended he was doing Dany a favour. (Maniacal Jasmine wanted to videotape their tryst, but he said no. See what a good friend he was?)

The Yellowknife movie, a low-budget thriller called *Sédentaire,* had unexpectedly won the audience award at the Festival des films du monde. Since then, Dany often invited Benoit to play pool at the Ombilic, ostensibly out of friendship ("Man, we never get together anymore"), but maybe also to show off, because someone would inevitably slap Dany on the back and applaud his success. Already Benoit had spotted two women at a nearby table goading each other to get Dany's autograph.

"So what are you doing with your mentee?" Dany asked, after leaning over the table and banking a shot into a pocket.

"Something light," Benoit said. "A comedy piece."

He still hadn't made up his mind about *Jaybird*. He'd been thinking maybe he and Madeleine should take a crack at comedy instead.

"You're doing light comedy?"

"Why not?"

"Not your forte, Ben," Dany said. "You can do the drug dealer, the narcissistic model or the mental retard. You've got those roles down pat. But making people laugh, forget it."

At this point, Dany's two fans butted in. They shook their skunky streaked hair. Benoit went to the bar for a drink. Dany was right; he *was* limited to specific roles. Dany, on the other hand, was not. Odd thing about Dany: in real life, he was a ham, he over-acted, but on stage or film, he could do anything. Move you, electrify or terrorize you, get you weeping, chuckling, get you on his side. It had always been that way, even back when they were twelve years old and Dany and his family shared a duplex in Anjou with Benoit and his parents.

Benoit watched Dany lean over the pool table to sign a napkin. The start of a gut protruded in his T-shirt. Benoit pictured himself yanking up Dany's shirt and dotting his friend's belly with Magic Marker. "No nudity for you," he'd say. "Not your forte, Dan."

He thought of his nude scene in *Jaybird*. His ass in the spotlight. Madeleine's skin, as smooth and white as a bar of soap. While the others limped their feeble Lauras across the stage, he and Madeleine could strip down. Delve into extremes. Jolt the audience.

He'd do it.

Still, Benoit had a niggling feeling about *Jaybird*. Years ago, while driving in the country, he'd seen a hawk get electrocuted atop a telephone poll. The thing thudded to the ground like a bag of garbage. As Benoit drove past, a wing lifted feebly and waved goodbye.

He didn't want *Jaybird* jolting him. He wanted to trust this Madeleine character and thought seeing her in her own habitat might help. So he stopped by Agence Wingood unannounced. The agency was in a greystone that had once been a bed and breakfast.

The lobby was done in dark oak. It included a reading nook set up in a bay window, where, the day he dropped in, the receptionist was serving celebrated author-playwright Pierre Saint-Michel a plate of cookies and a glass of milk. Benoit smiled at the man, who was too intent on his snack to notice.

"I got you the chewy cookies," the receptionist said.

"I like chewy," Pierre Saint-Michel said. "Yummy yum yums."

Benoit wandered down the hall, looking for Madeleine. Along the wall were headshots of Wingood's more famous clients. He wasn't among them, and the last time he was here neither was Dany Savard, but now Dany's asymmetrical face stared out from the wall. A woman carrying a coffeepot walked by and pointed out Madeleine's office, the last door on his left. He knocked on a pane of frosted glass.

"Yes."

He opened the door. Madeleine sat at her desk with a headset banded through her hair and the microphone hovering near her mouth like a tiny spaceship.

"I thought we'd rehearse at my place tonight," he said from the doorway. He'd originally booked the Confiserie from seven to nine, but now that he'd decided to give the jaybird wing, he didn't want any mentor or mentee getting a peek at the sketch before its unveiling. "That way, we'll keep our surprise under wraps."

"Sounds swell," she said. The telephone rang. She pressed a button on the phone and held up one finger at Benoit.

"Madeleine speaking."

He wondered if she had a boyfriend. He could picture one. An engineer with bad posture and acne scars. On the wall was a laminated poster, a beach scene of white parasols stuck into white sand. RAPTURES ON THE RIVIERA, Benoit read. Maybe the boyfriend had taken her there. Maybe the boyfriend had dumped her and caused a stewing anger that spawned *Jaybird*. Maybe it was none of his business.

She wrapped up her phone conversation. "I could bring some sandwiches tonight if you want."

"It's a date, then," he said. He began reciting his address, but she cut in. "I've got it on file."

The actress Pascale Chastenay came down the hall and stood in the doorway beside Benoit. "Knock knock," she said.

"Who's there?" Benoit said, but she ignored him. She had a regal forehead and bee-stung lips. She had two Gémeaux Awards and two Masques for best stage actress.

"Has the reporter from *Lundi* magazine arrived yet?" she asked Madeleine.

The look Madeleine threw Pascale was just like the puzzled stare in Benoit's repertoire of expressions. "That interview's at their office," Madeleine said. "Not ours."

"What! Oh, for God's sake, you told me *here*."

"I said *their* office."

"I know my possessive adjectives, Madeleine. You said *our* office."

"I even gave you their address," Madeleine muttered. She turned and began clicking her mouse. Pages of a calendar appeared on her computer monitor.

Pascale turned to Benoit. He'd heard she'd just finished directing her first documentary, apparently about landmine amputees. "There are days I could just pistol-whip some people," she said. "You know what I mean, Bernard?"

He didn't correct his name. He didn't say anything.

Madeleine jotted something on a slip of paper. "Here's the address," she said, handing Pascale the paper. "I'll call a cab to zoom you right over there."

"Yeah, well, I'm not shelling out for cab fare," Pascale said.

"I hear you, honey," Madeleine said.

Benoit said, "I better get going, Madeleine."

She strained a smile. "Yeah, see ya, Bernard."

He headed back down the hall. He'd wanted to see

Madeleine in a setting more real than the Confiserie, but Agence Wingood, with its frosted glass and hallway of headshots, was just as make-believe.

"I'm very grouchy if somebody gives me a hard cookie," the author-playwright said just before Benoit swung out the front door. As he descended the stone steps, Wingood emerged from a cab. The skin on her face had the taut, slightly creased look of saran wrap stretched over a bowl. The day he'd signed his agency contract, she'd flashed him the face-lift scars behind her ears. "If they don't heal before the Gémeaux Awards show," she told him, "I'll slice that surgeon's face off with a butter knife."

Today Wingood wore a tailored suit and had her bone white hair styled wispy. She was sixty-eight years old. Actors called her either by her last name only (like a football player) or "Mommy" (given her penchant for the word "motherfucker").

"I pulled a string or two to get Madeleine into Mentorat," she said to Benoit, grasping his arm with a rakish hand. "She especially wanted to work with you. Hope she hasn't got the hots. Though come to think of it, she isn't the type."

"What type is she?"

"Smart as a whip. Been with me ten years. A photographic memory. Listens good." Wingood stared at him sternly. "Anybody screws with her head and I'll break their motherfucking arm." She gave Benoit's arm a feeble squeeze. "Got it?"

"Got it."

"So what sketch are you two doing?"

"A scene from *Je hèle un taxi*," he lied.

"The cabbie who runs over the kid?"

"Yep."

"Safe choice."

At that point, Pascale Chastenay came running down the stone steps, yelling, "Taxi! Taxi!" but Wingood's cab drove off without her.

At night, the fountain in Parc Lafontaine changed colours every five minutes. For now, the water shooting out the top was orange-red and sprayed like sparks from a welder's torch. At the foot of the fountain, visible in the dim light, were dozens of ducks gliding across the man-made pond. One was big and Donald Duck white. Its size and whiteness reminded Benoit of Madeleine.

The two of them were sitting on a boulder alongside the pond, the rose-patterned hat box between them. It was ten o'clock, a warm night in late September. After they'd rehearsed *Jaybird* in his loft, he'd offered to walk her to her apartment building off the park and, along the way, they'd stopped at the fountain. In the dim light from the lamp posts, he could see that she'd missed a few Magic Marker lines on her neck (after their rehearsal, she pulled out a container of diaper wipes from her hat box and used them to erase the blue lines). He wondered again what had driven her to cook up such a perverse sketch, but unaccustomed to asking others about their lives, he talked about himself. His career. HIS CAREER! He half-joked that the characters from the plays and shows he did hunkered down in his head and began berating him: When would he land a meaty TV role? Get a lucrative commercial? Bag a Gémeaux? Stop asking his mother for money? "Their voices whisper in my ear. They're making me schizo, man."

She turned from the fountain, her face inscrutable. "So, honey, what are the characters in *Jaybird* telling you?"

Benoit foraged around in the hat box and pulled out the rubber mask. He slipped his fist inside. "Well, Nancy's telling me to head for the hills"—he held the mask like a hand puppet and tried working its lips with his fingers—"because that Madeleine chick's a loon."

"That Nancy chick's a wise woman," Madeleine said, sticking a finger into the mask's mouth hole and tickling his palm. Weirdly erotic. He thought of the blowjob mouths of inflatable sex dolls.

"Nancy wants to know if Madeleine ever studied dance."

His fingers clamped her fingernail till she yanked the mask from his hand and balled it up in her lap.

"I got fitted for my first tutu at eight."

"How long did you study?"

"Twelve years."

"Did you get anywhere with it?"

She gazed at the fountain. The spray turned the blue of natural gas. "Yeah, I got to the point where I knew I wouldn't get anywhere with it."

"You're really good."

She looked directly at him. "I'm too old and too fat. And even when I was younger and thinner, I was only ever mediocre."

"I bet you were better than you think."

"No, Benoit, I was ordinary." Her voice was different. Less cheery, more honest. "But that's okay. Sometimes we gotta accept our ordinariness and move on."

He sat watching the ducks and considering his career. The excruciating auditions. The bayonet of rejections. The measly pay. The buzz he no longer got from seeing his name on a theatre program. The years it took to finally become an up-and-comer.

"Wingood says you're a big asset," he said to take his mind off himself. "You've got an elephant's memory."

Madeleine sniggered. "Can you keep a big secret?"

He nodded.

"Sugar, I never forget dates, appointments or auditions because I've hooked up a tiny tape recorder to my phone. I record everything." She gave him a look of private hilarity. "Say I forget where and when Benoit Doré is auditioning for the show *Dossier criminel.* Well, I just listen to my trusty tape."

"That's your big secret? I bet you've got bigger ones."

"We're not supposed to record, so mum's the word to Mommy Wingood."

He silenced himself by pinching his mouth between two fingers.

She smirked. "You look like a duck."

A German shepherd bounded down the hill toward the pond. Its guttural woofs had the ducks paddling away or taking wing. All except the big white duck. It honked and stared the dog down.

"Courageous bird," Benoit said.

A teenager called the dog back and leashed its collar.

"It's a domestic duck somebody abandoned here," Madeleine said. "Happens every year. When all the others fly south, it'll stay put. It'll freeze or starve to death." From her hat box, she pulled out half a leftover peanut butter and banana sandwich, peeled off a length of crust and tossed the strip into the water. The white duck made a beeline.

"Poor stupid bird," she said.

Earlier in the evening, they had rehearsed *Jaybird* at Benoit's loft. After they'd eaten their sandwiches, granola bars and individual strawberry yogurts (the supper she'd brought was like a school kid's brown bag), Benoit went into the bathroom and took off his clothes. He stood in front of the mirror in his white jockeys (for their rehearsals, Madeleine suggested keeping their underwear on). He pressed his palms together in an isometric prayer intended to puff out his pecs. With a disposable Bic, he shaved the odd hair sprouting around his nipples.

He'd been nude onstage only once. In *Comme par hasard,* he and Lucie Faucher had to slide naked out of bed and slip on housecoats. But with the lighting so subdued and the bed so far upstage, the audience couldn't even tell, as Lucie Faucher pointed out, whether he was cut or uncut.

He opened the bathroom door. Madeleine was sitting on his sofa, dimpled knees crossed.

She stood. She was naked.

He blinked his eyes over her body. Her breasts were

small but the nipples long. Her pubic hair was dark red like saffron.

"I decided, Fuck the undies," she said.

He'd turned down all the lights in his loft, except those above his makeshift stage. There he stood, holding up a hand mirror to see behind him where Madeleine held a second mirror, his wood-framed one, over her belly. In her mirror was his ass. It looked so freakish, floating where her stomach should be, as if she'd swallowed it. When he'd first dropped his drawers, he'd felt sexy, seductive. Now he felt ludicrous. Whenever she said something like "Now jut out your left cheek," he'd giggle.

"It's okay. You're doing fine. Thataboy!"

Her tone—like a mom teaching her son to ride a bike—made him laugh harder. "This'll be my first comedy number," he said. "And comedy's not my forte."

Oh God, what was he doing? Would she make him look like a fool?

"So people might laugh. That's good. The humour will be offset in Act II," Madeleine said, setting her mirror down. "But do it right and it won't be vulgar. Pretend you're Michelangelo's *David*, and the audience will be seduced by the beauty of your ass. The women will. The men, too. Because it's a beautiful thing, an ass is."

I'm a beautiful ass, he thought.

"Let's go again," she said, lifting the mirror back up. "Pretend your butt's belly-dancing."

He started swinging his hips. She started humming Van Morrison's "Moondance," and he snorted.

"More extreme," she said impatiently. "You're not being extreme enough."

Benoit had the marker out and was skipping it across her upper arm. He smelled the flowery scent of her shampoo. A line she'd suggested in her script came to mind. "The sexual fantasies of ugly girls never star themselves," he sneered.

"Keep going," she said from beneath her Nancy face. "The nastier you are, the easier it is."

He didn't know if the rubber mask helped. The smiling vacuity of it. Through the nickel-size holes in Nancy's eyes, he glimpsed Madeleine's eyes. He felt like a pervert serial killer. He stood close to mark up her other arm, and his dick grazed her thigh.

"Nastier!"

"I can't," he mumbled. His marker hovered over her shoulder. Perfect skin: not one freckle, not one mole.

"Christ, honey," she pleaded. "Please do this for me."

What had made her this way? Who'd hurt her?

"Pretty please."

"Okay, okay," he said. He thought up an original insult. Hollered it: "You think a guy can pop a boner around you? No fucking way. You, lady, are a boner deflator."

In his head, a curtain unravelled to the stage: the end.

Madeleine yanked off her Nancy head. Smiled. "Jesus, Benoit, that was a good one."

He watched her. He lay on his cork floor in his plaid bathrobe, a cushion propped under his head. Tchaikovsky's "*Scène dansante*" played on his stereo. The sofa and coffee table were pushed against the window. The curtains were drawn. The curtains were made of a mesh flyswatter-like material. See-through. Anyone standing in the courtyard below wouldn't see him lying on the floor but might make out the white blur of Madeleine.

She was whirling around the room. Pirouetting past his *Ficus carica*. Legs extended. Arms floating.

Graceful. Elegant. Delicate. Lovely.

ACT II: THE HUMILIATION

How come the École nationale de théâtre offered no courses on handling humiliation with grace? After all, for an actor in Montreal, the risk of degradation was high. Benoit knew this. And so far, he'd counted himself lucky. He hadn't yet needed to fake awe and reverence in an infomercial for non-stick cookware. He hadn't yet acted in Agatha Christie's *Dix petits nègres* in, God help him, some suburban dinner theatre. No voice-over work for porno. No guest-starring on the game show *La tête cassée*, where contestants tackled such brainteasers as the chemical formula for water.

By sticking to productions at Montreal's downtown theatres—the Confiserie, the Licorne, the Rideau Vert, the Quat'Sous, Espace Go, Usine C—he'd managed to elude the worst humiliations. Not to say that all the plays he acted in were magnum opuses. Some were pretentious, others lethargic, dull. One reviewer, who fled early, wrote that had she been handcuffed to her seat, she'd have gladly chewed through her arm to escape Act II of *La fumerie d'opium*. Still, in general, the plays he starred in fared well and earned him some laudatory reviews and even a nomination at the Masque Awards. What these roles didn't earn him was a living.

How humiliating was it for Benoit, at age twenty-nine, to drop by one of his parents' health food stores (they now had four of them: Grün, Verde, Groen, Viridis) to pick up a cheque to tide him over? His mother or father always passed him the cheque, sealed in a manila envelope, as furtively as in a drug transaction. In exchange, he occasionally helped out at Verde. Which wasn't so humiliating given that *Voir* magazine hailed him as "an emerging talent humble enough to do a price check on a tub of tofu."

So far in Benoit's acting life, what was most humiliating was the pecking order, specifically his place in it. He hadn't yet graduated to television. (He'd done some film work, but with the local market so small, no Montreal actor lived off films). He was a rooster in a cage marked THEATRE and above him was another cage labelled TELEVISION whose roosters kept crapping on his head.

To make a living, he needed TV.

The day after Madeleine danced in his apartment, Benoit auditioned as a mellow cop for a four-episode arc in the TV program *Dossier criminel.* The casting director yelled, "Excellent!" at the end of one scene when he threw a lady cop a beatific smile. He'd borrowed that smile from Madeleine's blissful ballerina.

When he got home, he called Madeleine at the agency. "The show's mediocre. The writing's mediocre.

The directing's mediocre. And my acting was damn mediocre," he said. "So I fit in well."

"Sometimes mediocrity's besides the point."

"What's with the words of wisdom?" he teased. "According to Mentorat, I'm the one mentoring you."

"There's no mentor," she said. "Just two rats."

The frustration over his audition began a slow fade as they talked and joked. She mentioned that she couldn't rehearse that night, as she was helping someone move. Who, he didn't ask. He knew the colour of her pubic hair but couldn't ask her a personal question. Maybe her engineer boyfriend was moving in with her. The one with the zits.

"Besides, we shouldn't overwork *Jaybird*," she said. "We've got to be spontaneous. We've got to improvise."

That night, he wiggled his ass in front of a mirror and spent ten minutes yelling abuse from the Duo-Tang script. "The pores on your nose look like the dimples on golf balls!" Later he ordered in some Indian curries, and as he was tossing the empty cartons in the trash, he spotted the bunched-up diaper wipes Madeleine had rubbed over her skin to erase the Magic Marker. They were smudged blue. He picked a few from the trash and sniffed them. Baby powder and witch hazel.

He pictured her white skin. The give of her flesh as he pressed down with his pen. The rose petal pink island of skin around her nipples. Her nipples stiffening. His dick brushing her thigh. The peekaboo flash of her vagina as she lay beside his *Ficus elastica,* swishing her legs in the air.

He crouched right there on his kitchen floor and jerked off into the blue diaper wipes.

Afterwards, he went for a walk up rue Saint-Denis. He passed boutiques selling hemp bedclothes, African tribal masks, scented soaps, teak patio furniture. Though it was eleven o'clock, people still streamed by. He stopped in front of a shop selling clothing for fat ladies. In the window were posters of models, plumped-up versions of the skinny girls from fashion magazines. Same gleaming skin, shiny hair, sparkly eyes. They did not have Madeleine's sunken eyes. They did not have her recklessness, her secretiveness, her hurt.

Back at his building around midnight, he saw from the courtyard that the lights were on in his loft. He had turned them off. He sprinted up the stairs, thinking—illogically, since she didn't have a key—that she might be waiting.

Dany blubbered, his nose snotty and his face more off kilter than usual. Benoit sat beside him on the sofa, patting him between the shoulder blades—slow, even taps as if Dany were a baby with gas.

Dany's girlfriend had finally dumped him.

He'd always been a show-stopping weeper. In eighth grade, when Dany's parents had announced their divorce, Benoit had sat on a sofa in Dany's panelled rec room, burping his friend as he bawled.

"I can't, I can't, I can't, I can't–" Dany babbled now. He clutched a cushion, rocked forward.

Benoit whispered, "Can't what, man?"

"Dunno, dunno, dunno, dunno–"

Eventually, Benoit went to the kitchen nook to brew a pot of brown-rice tea. Not till Dany was sipping his tea and said, "Jasmine drinks this shit," did Benoit remember she'd left Calm Zen in his pantry during their affair last year.

Around two in the morning, Benoit and Dany called it a night. Dany lay on the sofa under a cotton blanket, while Benoit climbed into his bed. On the ceiling above the bed hung heavy curtains on a circular track. Benoit usually drew them around the bed at night–it felt like sleeping onstage–but tonight Dany had asked him not to.

Benoit said, "Us lying in the dark reminds me of the fort."

A snort from Dany.

Back in eighth grade, they'd had a peculiar urban fort: a mountain of beanbag chairs heaped together within a corral enclosure at the Mail d'Anjou near their duplex. Once the mall's employees and customers were distracted, they'd dive into the beanbags and tunnel through to the dark air pockets that formed in the pile.

"You'd make me crack up in there, imitating the vice-principal, our gym teacher, your little sister." Benoit missed those times. Back then, he worshipped Dany. He hadn't yet begun the gruelling chore of trying to outdo him.

"God, you were hilarious."

"Ben?" Dany's voice was a ping in the darkness.

"Yeah?"

"Can I ask you something?"

He'd deny it. If Dany asked if he'd ever screwed Jasmine, he'd say no.

"You ever get lonely?"

A pause. Then: "Sure, man, like everybody."

"'Cause sometimes, Ben, I feel like the last slug on Earth after a nuclear fallout. You know?"

"Yeah, I do."

They were lonesome slugs. The pair of them. Self-obsessed, vain, sickly competitive. Benoit knew this. No surprise they couldn't hang on to girlfriends. Staring across at the green digits keeping time on his microwave, he imagined Madeleine's cool, white body lying against his under the covers. In his twenty-nine years, he'd had thirty-two girlfriends, starting with pragmatic but aloof Danielle (who'd open his canned puddings for him in grade two) and ending last month with Hélène (a compulsive liar he'd twice caught pocketing other people's tips when the two of them ate out in restaurants). He fell asleep dreaming that all his exgirlfriends were heaped into the beanbag corral and he was looking for a spot where he could burrow in.

He was woken at 5:35 by a gentle knocking on his front door. Hair on end, mouth sour with the morningafter taste of Calm Zen, army camouflage pants pulled on to camouflage his morning boner, he went to answer the door, but it swung open before he got there. In walked Jasmine.

Damn. Why had he given sets of keys to these people? To water his ficus when he'd been in Louisiana last winter. And had they watered them? Barely. He'd come home to find the leaves of his *Ficus benjamina* scattered all over the floor.

"How's Sonny Boy?" Jasmine whispered. She and Benoit sometimes pretended they were divorced parents with joint custody of Dany.

"Sleeping like a baby," Benoit said. In the background, Dany's light snoring sounded like a cooing pigeon.

"A colicky baby, I bet," Jasmine said. She was wearing cycling shorts. She must have biked over.

She had the sinewy body of the former professional cyclist she was. She brushed past, scarcely looking at Benoit. Ever since they'd slept together, eye contact had been condensed to a blink or two.

She knelt in front of the sofa and whispered, "Hey, Snorkeldorf." When Dany opened his eyes, he gave her an ingenuous smile, which then wilted as he awakened to the facts: the breakup, Benoit's lumpy couch.

The two of them went and holed up in the bathroom, the only private place in the loft, while Benoit lay on his bed, the curtains drawn around him. He put his Walkman on and listened to a new CD he'd just bought: Tchaikovsky's dance themes. As the melody bounced from strings to woodwinds, Benoit recalled the last time he'd seen Jasmine. They were at a bash she'd thrown at her and Dany's apartment to celebrate the best-actor Masque that Dany had copped for *Juste un petit malaise.* Halfway through the raucous party, Benoit slid out to the back balcony for some peace, and there was Jasmine, sitting alone on the fire escape and downing a Cape Cod. "Sonny Boy won a gold star," she said to him.

"He's made his dad proud," he said. To avoid looking at her, he stared at the glowing red Crowne Plaza sign atop a hotel up the street.

Soon Dany's notorious throttled-chicken yodel came from inside the apartment, and Jasmine caught

Benoit's eye and said wearily, "Well, he's made his mom so jealous she could spit." Then she horked over the fire escape and onto the windshield of a car parked below.

Benoit smirked. He felt the same phlegmy envy. What a wretched friend he was. Hateful. No one needed to tell him that. "One day Children's Aid is gonna learn what rotten parents we are," he said, "and Sonny Boy'll be carted off to foster care."

Jasmine got up and hooked her arm through his— the first time she'd touched him since they'd fucked— and together they strode back into the party, Jasmine whispering, "Happy thoughts, happy thoughts."

Now, lying on his bed, Benoit tried thinking happy thoughts. He thought of Madeleine. Her tippytoe jetés. They brought a smile to his face.

As he was humming along to *Le lac des cygnes,* the curtain around his bed pulled back. Dany jumped on the bed, a golden retriever in boxer shorts. When he grabbed Benoit by the shoulders, Benoit thought, Jesus, she's spilled the beans, but Dany simply yanked out Benoit's earphones and kissed him, two big smackeroos, on the crown of his head. "We're giving it another shot, man," he said. Then he leapt around the loft, tugging on his pants and shoes, while Jasmine went downstairs to wait.

———

On Friday evening, at an hour when a broken dinner plate of a moon was visible against a blue sky, Benoit took a cab at Madeleine's request to rue Champagne. The name sounded festive. Pop and fizz. But it was a decrepit street with a peeling Seventh-day Adventist church across from a basement soup kitchen run by the same order of nuns Mother Teresa had belonged to. As he paid the cabbie, a nun biked by in her blue-trimmed white sari and sandals. Madeleine sat on a stoop in front of a block-long expanse of row houses, their top windows boxed into dormers.

After the cab drove off, she led him behind these houses, her nylon exercise pants swishing as she walked. They entered a paved alleyway bordered by small fenced-in backyards. Someone was stringing laundry on a line. Someone else was scraping charred meat from a barbecue. Two tabby cats as fat as raccoons wriggled under a fence. The fruit from a crabapple tree bounced off a Jetta pimpled with rust. Above all this, squirrels tightrope-walked the phone lines.

Madeleine set her hat box down in a pothole. She told Benoit her family had lived on rue Champagne till she was fifteen. "When I was a kid, this was my theatre," she said, opening her arms wide like an opera singer. "I love making up lives for the people around me. I did it for our neighbours. For instance, in the yard over there was a guy with a dyed pompadour and a tattoo of a tear dripping from one eye. For me, he wasn't a Hydro repairman with the DTs. He was Blue Suede Shoes, a crooner who sang off-key at weddings and bar mitzvahs."

Benoit set her boom box down at his feet. "Have you made up a life for me?"

"What do you think *Jaybird* is?" She smiled slyly and then drifted along the alley. She pointed to a third-floor balcony in the middle of the row houses where a woman in a tube top sat reading. "That's where I used to live. That balcony was my box seat."

Benoit looked around. The alleyway, with balconies on both sides, *was* a kind of agora theatre. Madeleine's idea was to rehearse there, a dry run with their clothes on. So Benoit did his little dance, aiming his ass brashly at the woman on her balcony. Afterwards, he circled Madeleine, sweeping his capped marker through the air. He kept his voice down so no one puttering around in the yards would hear. "Your tits are cockeyed: one looks east, the other west." He took out the rubber Nancy mask and began sliding it over her hair. She must have been chewing her lips, because the skin was really chapped; it looked like mica flakes. Maybe she had butterflies, what with *Jaybird* debuting in two days. His heart twinged. He felt protective, a real mentor like that old bearded guy from *Odyssée*. "Don't worry," he said. "On Sunday, you're gonna kick everybody's ass."

With the deflated Nancy head perched crazily atop her own head, she muttered, "I know."

He pulled the mask all the way down and kissed the crown of that rubber head twice. Two smackeroos.

She danced along the alleyway with Tchaikovsky on her boom box, turned down low. Afterwards, they trampled the long grass beside the rusty Jetta and plopped themselves down. Madeleine mopped her sweaty forehead with a diaper wipe and then handed him another peanut butter and banana sandwich from her hat box. She twiddled the radio dial on her boom box to a classical station and hummed along as they chewed on their sandwiches.

Madeleine could have gotten Wingood to pair her with Georges Valiquette or Lucie Faucher or any one of the more illustrious mentors. But she'd chosen him.

"You picked me because I've got balls," he said, repeating what she'd said the first night at the Confiserie.

"Also because you're young, sugar. There's still time for you to become somebody."

"A star?" he scoffed.

She looked at him. "No, a real person."

"Rather than?"

"A figment."

"What, of my own imagination?"

"Or maybe of mine."

He assumed she meant acting was all pretend. Some actors—Dany, for example—claimed that playing different characters let them explore emotional channels and sides of their personality they didn't realize existed. But no matter which role Benoit played—crack dealer, mentally retarded paperboy, mellow cop—he never felt that way. He always felt spurious. A six-year-old awarded three quarters for his bogus smile.

"You're young, too," he repeated to Madeleine.

"I'm thirty-six."

"Are you happy with the somebody you've become?"

She glanced around. Looked up at the box seat where she once kept watch, inventing stories about the people around her. "Not yet," she said. "But I'm getting there."

They shared a cab back to the Plateau, the hat box and boom box between them on the seat. She was to get out on boulevard Saint-Laurent to take care of some business. "I'm still in the midst of my move," she explained.

"Oh, are *you* moving? I thought you were helping a friend move."

"Hey, there goes Dany Savard," Madeleine said. The cab was stopped at a light, and Dany was crossing the street, one arm slung over Jasmine's shoulders, mashing her against him so that they looked like partners in a three-legged race.

"Attractive couple."

"Yep," he muttered.

"Dany seems like a nice guy."

"He's a good actor."

It was Sunday night, show time, and Dany was onstage, a beheaded glass unicorn in his hand. As always, he was eloquent, he was poignant. For Christ's sake, he made Benoit want to weep. However, Dany's mentee, playing the lame Laura, hobbled around as if her leg were clenched by a rabid poodle.

For the special one-night performance of Mentorat, the Confiserie had sold out, all twenty rows of seats filled. Benoit sat in the fourth row, Madeleine beside him, her white hands resting on her knees like balls of dough.

That afternoon, they'd staged a quick dress rehearsal fully dressed with only the lighting technician present. Madeleine had spent most of the rehearsal blasting her boom box. She'd plunked in the Tchaikovsky cassette and then turned it over to play a recording of her own voice repeating: "Madeleine speaking. Madeleine speaking. Madeleine speaking."

A kind of testing, testing, one, two, three.

Intermission. Five of the sketches had been performed, the most inventive being Cécile Bellehumeur and her male apprentice dolled up like drag queens to play a feuding Mary Stuart and Elizabeth I. Five more sketches would come after the half-hour break, with *Jaybird* first up.

In the lobby of the Confiserie, Benoit wedged through the crowd in search of Madeleine. He'd lost her backstage. When last he'd seen her, she was at the props table, fiddling with the clasp on her hat box. She looked ashen. Scared stiff. For a second, he thought, Shit, she's gonna bolt out of here. He went for a pee, and when he came out of the washroom he couldn't find her.

People in the lobby were sipping wine and nibbling finger foods. Pita triangles and dip. Fried zucchini sticks. Tiny carrot stumps like orange suppositories. Cécile Bellehumeur arrived in her wig and pancake makeup. Luc Bourguignon was there with his uproarious laugh, a hyena on nitrous oxide. At the bar, surly Georges Valiquette was getting tanked again.

"Happy birthday!"

"Happy ten years!"

"Happy anniversary!"

"Happy first decade!"

Benoit craned his neck. No Madeleine.

Out of the crowd came Dany. "Here's my man!" Dany cried and toasted the air with his glass of wine.

Beside him was Jasmine. She looked at Benoit with heavy-lashed eyes, as beautiful as a cow's. Cupped in her hand was a clump of carrot stumps. "Hey," she mumbled and gnawed a carrot.

"Thanks again, buddy, for the other night," Dany said. "You're a real friend, man."

Weird how whenever anyone told Benoit he was a real friend, he always felt he had not a friend in the world.

"Great performance, Dan," Benoit said. "Real touching."

Dany's face was shiny. The guy was gleaming. "You know, the only critic I care about is you, Ben. You're my most excellent audience." Dany's smile was as wide as a canoe. He had an announcement to make. Big, big news, he said. He'd just been cast in *Andromède,* a sci-fi flick to be filmed in France.

"Congrats, Dan."

"I swear, this'll be the role to break me."

"But, honey, you're already broken," Jasmine deadpanned.

Someone poked Benoit's shoulder. It was Wingood, dressed in a silver sheath, a small silver purse slung over her shoulder.

"Hi, Mommy!" Dany said. "Did I do good? You know, the only critic I care about is you."

Wingood fixed Benoit with a grim stare. "Where is she?"

"Who?"

"Madeleine," Wingood said. "Who'd you think?"

He shrugged and scanned the crowd. Wingood shooed Dany and Jasmine away, saying she had private matters to thrash out with Benoit.

"Uh-oh, you're in trouble!" chanted Dany.

When they were gone, she clicked open her purse and pulled out a folded sheet of paper. "I dropped by the office before the show and found this on my desk. She's deserted me. Ten years of my paycheques, and she leaves me a one-line letter."

She thrust the letter at Benoit. *Dear Wingood,* he read, *This is my official resignation letter announcing I have officially resigned.* Madeleine's name and signature were at the bottom with a PS: *Keep my last paycheque as restitution.*

Wingood grabbed the letter back. "You lied to her that she had talent, didn't you?"

"She *is* talented," he said. "She's—"

"Yeah, right, if you tell me she's a born actress, I'm gonna puke on your shoes."

"I mean, she could be more than just a voice on my phone."

"She already is more than that. She's my friggin' right-hand man. You want the truth: she practically runs the joint. She's a born Wingood. So if you've filled her head with dreams of better, you're gonna suffer big time."

Backstage, pairs of mentees and mentors were donning costumes and smearing on makeup. The actor Yannick Cyr was decked out in a tuxedo. The actress Lucie Faucher wore a leather teddy. She told Benoit she'd just seen Madeleine go into a change room. "Thank fucking God," Benoit said. He went into his own change room and locked the door. He took off his clothes, checked his ass for pimples, mussed up his hair with mud putty, puffed out his chest with a few isometric exercises, beefed up his dick with a few yanks and then slipped on his ratty plaid bathrobe.

He found Madeleine back at the props table in a terrycloth robe. On the table sat her hat box and boom box, along with her folded jeans, her balled-up socks, her leather shoes. She was folding her blouse.

So she'd quit her job. Good for her. He'd wait till the show was over to ask about her plans. Maybe after their performance, they'd ditch the lame Confiserie crowd and go for a drink. Leave everybody to pluck apart *Jaybird*.

"Did you remember to put new batteries in your ghetto blaster?"

Madeleine nodded. She kept unfolding and refolding her blouse. She avoided looking at him. Stage fright, he assumed. He took the blouse from her and laid it on the table. He had her close her eyes and then grasped her hands. Her palms were clammy. Recalling the French Riviera poster in her office, Benoit said, "Picture a sandy beach with white parasols. A sun like a peach. Lapping waves." This visualization calmed jitters, or so claimed one of his old acting coaches. He'd always found the exercise dopey, though, so he shut up and they simply stood together, eyes closed, hands clasped. He could hear members of the audience settling down, coughing. Madeleine's breath through her nose whistled faintly.

She was the only woman he'd ever brought home, got naked with and not screwed.

He pictured them lying naked on his bed, the curtains drawn around them. He was teasing her nipples erect with a moist toilette smudged blue.

When the stagehand gave them their cue, they pulled apart. "Break a leg," Benoit said.

"I will." Her small eyes were as round and shiny as dimes. "I'll break them both."

At age fifteen, he'd spent one sweltering July night alone at his uncle's cottage on a private lake. At three a.m., his face swampy with sweat, he went down to the dock and threw off his clothes. The full moon reflected in the black water as if it had fallen from the sky and sunk to the lake bottom. He dove toward the moon. His first time skinny-dipping. He felt an intense, thundering thrill. For the first time in his life, Benoit Doré felt virile. Sexy.

On the stage of the Confiserie, that deep exhilaration and that July night came back to him as a cone of light shone on his ass. He bucked his hips and clenched his muscles. No one was laughing. The audience was pin-drop silent. Van Morrison's "Moondance" hummed in his head. It was time for romance. For him and his love.

When the lights turned up, Madeleine toddled out onstage. She was fully dressed. Jeans, blouse, shoes. DRESSED! SHE WAS FULLY DRESSED! His back still to the audience, he bugged his eyes out at her. For fuck sake, she'd lost her nerve. She'd yellow-bellied.

He was twisting his face. What now? What now? But she looked terrifyingly cool. She set her boom box down mid-stage and walked over. "You have to trust me," she whispered. She bent down and unclasped the top of her hat box. No Magic Marker, no Nancy mask, no diaper wipes, no sandwiches for later. Instead he saw silver: shiny handcuffs, a large pair of scissors, a roll of duct tape. Feeling doomed, helpless, he let her push his legs together and hook cuffs around his ankles. She turned him around. The entire audience glanced at his full frontal. He could feel their eyes through the lights. He closed his eyes as she cuffed his hands behind his back. Someone coughed. Someone snorted. When someone gasped, he blinked his eyes open. Madeleine was crouched, scissors in hand. His hips recoiled. She snipped off a length of grey tape the size of a dollar bill, and he thought, Jesus Christ, she's gonna stick it on my dick.

She stood.

"Don't!"

It was the only line he'd deliver that night.

"I'm sorry," she whispered, but her eyes didn't look sorry. They looked ecstatic.

She taped his mouth.

Then she kissed his mouth. One big smackeroo.

———

Jaybirds weren't naked. They were covered in blue and white feathers. This idea came back to him as he lay onstage, one side of his face flattened against the floor, his nostrils filled with the gluey smell of the tape over his mouth. Beside him, in her blue jeans and white blouse, was Madeleine. They lay like two people in bed, the boom box their headboard. Benoit on his stomach, Madeleine on her back. She had ordered him down. In his cuffs, he'd gotten to his knees but then toppled over, bashing his shoulder. It now ached, but he paid it little attention. He was absorbed by Madeleine. Her eyes were shut. Her eyelids fluttered. Her face contorted. Her body writhed. Soft moans came from her throat. Nobody heard these moans, though. Nobody but him. The voices coming from the boom box drowned her out.

A minute earlier, from the floor where he'd fallen, he'd watched her press Play.

The flip side of Tchaikovsky.

"Madeleine speaking. Madeleine speaking. Madeleine speaking. Madeleine speaking . . ."

Two words. Ten times. Different tones.

Her overture.

Following this were snippets of conversations, mostly monologues by different actors interrupted by

Madeleine saying, "I hear you, honey" or "Good point" or "Sugar, you know what's best."

The first voice was Pascale Chastenay looking for a disease to become the spokeswoman for. "Nothing gross, though," she said. "AIDS isn't gross anymore. I'd do AIDS, but nothing like colon cancer where people crap in bags stapled to their stomach." Next up was Georges Valiquette grumbling about the bad press African genocides get when everybody knows they curb unbridled population growth and prevent starving. "It's rabbits and foxes out there," he insisted, "and right now there are too many rabbits."

The audience snorted, snickered, hooted.

Benoit, his shoulder throbbing, his dick crushed against the floor, felt trampled. He bored his eyes into Madeleine, but she wouldn't look his way. She was staring at the lighting equipment overhead. She moaned louder.

This woman's big secret: she recorded phone calls.

Her voice on the tape asked Luc Bourguignon where he'd be vacationing. "As if I'd tell you," Luc Bourguignon shot back. He accused her of an ulterior motive: wanting to sell the information to the tabloids. "I don't need paparazzi hanging out in my hotel lobby!" After a hissy fit, he made a sheepish apology. "I'm taking mother to Toronto," he admitted.

Next was a string of clients yelling at Madeleine, one calling her a half-wit. Then came a series of one-liners, one actor badmouthing another: "Michel's an ass wipe." "Véronique's a frigid whale." "Pascale's an über-bitch." "Yannick's a Radio-Canada cocksucker."

The audience's laughter came like hiccups.

Benoit was sweating. His armpits stank like they did during sex. Could Madeleine smell him? She arched her neck back, spread her legs. Moaned loader.

If anyone accused him of being in the know, he'd deny it. He'd tell the truth. She'd hoodwinked him. Basically raped him. As this thought came to him, the conversation turned to rape. "If not for violent movies and video games, more women would get raped," Serge Labrecque claimed. "Fake violence gives men an outlet."

"An outlet?" Madeleine said on tape. "Like for an electric plug?"

"Yeah, like a socket that guys can plug into."

More chortles from the audience. Benoit rubbed his mouth against the stage floor to loosen the tape. If he could get it off, what would he say?

Dance for us, Madeleine. Just dance for us.

That's what he'd say.

"Hope I'm not being indiscreet, but have you ever considered a chin implant?"

Dance for us, Madeleine.

"The pores on your nose look like the dimples on golf balls."

Dance for us.

"You said my audition was at four. Well, guess what, retard, it was at two."

Dance for us.

He'd scream it. He'd order her to.

"Movie stars provide a service, Madeleine." It was Dany speaking. His pal Dany Savard. "We're stand-ins in the sexual fantasies of the ugly."

"Is that right?"

"Yes, yes, because homely people don't want to put themselves in the picture. Too much of a turnoff. So they pick an attractive star to make love *for* them."

"I don't understand," Madeleine said on tape. "I don't understand you at all."

On the stage floor, Madeleine was crying out. Benoit watched her buck her hips. Thrash and twist.

Dance for us, Madeleine.

One arm flailed back, knocking the boom box's volume to maximum. Dany's voice blared: "CONFIDE IN ME, MADELEINE." Benoit winced. Madeleine winced. "IN YOUR WILDEST, KINKIEST FANTASY, WHO'S YOUR STAND-IN? WHO'S DOING THE FUCKING FOR YOU?"

Madeleine gaped her mouth wide in an ugly monkey grimace as the boom box let out a climatic, eardrum-cleaving screech.

On the floor of the change room, Benoit sat in his bathrobe, his back against the concrete wall and one hand fingering his sore jaw and the tackiness around his mouth left behind by the duct tape. Something was jabbing him in the thigh. He reached into his bathrobe pocket and pulled out the cassette. One side was neatly labelled JAYBIRD 1, the other JAYBIRD 2. He should crack the damn thing open. Rip the ribbon out. But he didn't. He stared at the cassette, at a small logo of a guy hunkered down in an armchair, his hair blown back by the gale force of whatever was coming out of his stereo speakers.

Benoit was that guy.

Only about a fifth of the tape had played. Maybe further on, she'd recorded a private message for him. An explanation. After the final screech, she had stood and walked offstage. Left him there. As he struggled to his knees, he fell, cracking his jaw on the floor. He curled up. The bloody audience applaud-ed. Wildly. There were whistles, bravos. Finally, Guy, the potbellied stagehand, appeared. He peeled the tape off Benoit's mouth, unlocked his cuffs and handed him his bathrobe. By this time, there was a standing ovation. Benoit nodded apathetically to the audience and got offstage.

In the wings, he said to the stagehand, "Where is she?"

"She hightailed it out the side door," Guy said. "But first she handed me some keys and said, 'Free the poor bastard.'" Guy was carrying the boom box. The cassette was unwinding silently in the machine.

At home that night, Benoit played "Jaybird 2" till the end, but it contained nothing more than a snaky background hiss.

He stockpiled the props. The second day after Mentorat, he returned to the Confiserie and absconded with the hat box (containing the scissors, duct tape, cuffs and keys) and the boom box. On the way home, he passed a drugstore window displaying Halloween costumes. A werewolf held a silver platter on which sat a decapitated Nancy head. He went in and bought the rubber mask. At home, he spread his spoil on his bed. He sat in his underpants. He locked and unlocked his feet in the ankle cuffs. Sniffed the gluey side of the duct tape. On the boom box, he played "Jaybird 1," the Tchaikovsky side. As for the other side of the cassette, he couldn't bring himself to listen to it again. Not yet. But he read the Duo-Tang script in search of clues.

Performing "Jaybird 1" had never been her intent, he supposed. It was a ruse designed to gain his trust and strip him down for the real show, "Jaybird 2." But why the ferocious insults? *That unused purse you couldn't give away at your garage sale, well, that was your pussy.*

"The nastier you are, the easier it is," she'd said.

The easier the betrayal?

He pulled the Nancy mask over his head and breathed in its rubbery condom smell. He recalled her dance. The splendour of it. She could have shown the audience that splendour, but she'd revealed it to him alone. Was her dance his compensation?

He'd been so stupid. A chump actor. A figment of this woman's imagination. There were moments he wanted to throttle her. She'd shackled and gagged him. His shoulder and jaw still hurt. But his anger abated a bit when he pictured her at home, stacks of cassettes on her desk, listening to hours of phone conversations and then editing together the plum parts. You had to admire her resolve. Her artistry and artfulness. Her revenge. He wished she'd played him "Jaybird 2" during their first rehearsal, asked his advice. Oh, but who was he fooling? He'd have balked: "I could lose work!" Maybe she'd realized this.

Maybe she'd kept him in the dark so he could later plead ignorance.

Too late to plead ignorance, though.

The first day after Mentorat, Benoit had gone to the pool hall to talk to Dany. "Jasmine always suspected you of being a backstabber," Dany said, "but I defended you: 'No, no, Ben's a good guy.'" Dany's eyes reddened, and Benoit expected him to get weepy again, but Dany just tap-tap-tapped his pool cue on the floor. "Tell me to my face you weren't in on that cow's stunt and I'll forgive you."

He'd planned to tell the truth, but now he couldn't. The truth seemed to him a lie. When he turned to leave, Dany jabbed the butt of the pool cue into the small of his back.

"Two-faced bastard," Dany muttered.

As Benoit walked down rue Saint-Denis, he glimpsed his face in a shop window. He recalled looking into his hand mirror and seeing his ass floating disembodied in Madeleine's stomach. His ass was his second face! He let out an embarrassed, disbelieving whoop of a laugh.

He made his way to the Agence Wingood. In the lobby, the receptionist called to him. He darted down the hall and threw open Wingood's office door as dramatically as an actor with one Masque nomination could. She peered over black-framed bifocals. "What do you want, Benoit?" she said in a tone more bored than peeved. "You want to know where she is? Well, we don't know. Your jaybird's flown the coop."

"I know."

First thing that morning, he'd gone to her apartment building and discovered from the concierge that she'd moved out the previous week. No forwarding address.

"I want to know *who* she is."

"Who she is?" Wingood took off her glasses and carefully folded them. "My dear boy, she's that girl in high school you flirted with so you could crib from her history essay. She's that cashier at Provigo you treat with as much humanity as a display of Shredded Wheat."

Benoit threw her his trademark: arresting glare through a flop of bangs.

Wingood inched up the cashmere sweater draped over her shoulders. She stared back. "Run along now," she said. "Mommy's got work to do."

Mediocrity was besides the point, Madeleine told him. She was right. He landed the job on the TV show *Dossier criminel*, although the mellow cop was rewritten. Dédé Rioux was now, according to his character description, "a handsome introvert, a recovering alcoholic, a young cop bent on revenge over the death of his beloved older brother, killed in a drug raid gone sour." After his four-episode arc, Dédé proved so popular that Benoit was signed as a regular.

In one episode, the dead brother popped up in a series of flashbacks. For the part, the show hired rising movie star Dany Savard. On the set, Dany shook Benoit's hand and then whacked him hard on the back. To the cast and crew, he announced, "Me and this guy are like this," and held up crossed fingers. "We're practically blood." Fitting, because in the drug-raid flashback, Benoit held a dying Dany and they bled fake blood on each other.

In a later episode, Dédé screwed a policewoman in the shower, flashing his butt across the TV screen. Soon thereafter, Benoit's headshot went up in the hallway at Agence Wingood.

"Why not just stick a shot of my ass up?" he said to Wingood as the receptionist hammered a nail into the wall.

"Don't be an ungrateful motherfucker," Wingood said. "I could have canned your ass, but I didn't."

Down the hall, he could hear the new girl on the phone. Her name was Hien, which, she'd told Benoit, meant "gentle" in Vietnamese. And she was gentle. Also chunky and walleyed. At the moment, Luc

Bourguignon was bullying her into babysitting his cat during his month-long shoot abroad. "Have I got this right?" Hien asked. "Minoune gets the kibble on weekdays and the canned on weekends?"

Other than his mug on the wall, nothing much had changed. *Jaybird* was soon forgotten. The story Wingood fed reporters was that the actors on the tape had recorded the dialogue, at Madeleine's request, expressly for her performance. In other words, they'd all been reading lines scripted by Madeleine for some satirical fantasy of hers.

In the evenings, while memorizing his lines in his loft, Benoit would sometimes play the tape everyone assumed had vanished along with Madeleine. His ears would block out the actors' voices and keep attuned only to Madeleine's sporadic remarks.

"Gosh, I hope so."

"No need to yell."

"Sugar, you know what's best."

As for her final line, he'd always recite it along with the tape.

"I don't understand you," they'd say in unison. "I don't understand you at all." And each time Benoit said it, he felt he understood Madeleine a tiny bit better.

ACT III: THE FANTASY

Whatever happened to Dédé Rioux? Four years after Benoit had quit *Dossier criminel*, a magazine phoned him to find out. "A feature in *Lundi* could be good for business," the reporter said. A few days later, she knocked on his door. Charlotte Dupuis had ironed-flat hair and a black velvet patch over one eye: a pretty woman with a pirate's face. "These are right out of *Alice au pays des merveilles*," she said as she flitted around his loft, examining the furniture Benoit had made. Most of the pieces were chests of drawers in pine or birch. Instead of clean, straight lines, they had curved sides and rounded corners. They were painted lime green, midnight blue and blood red.

"Some of the drawers don't slide out," he explained as Charlotte inspected a waist-high bureau. "You open the top drawer by flipping up the hinged top." He demonstrated. "You open the two bottom drawers by sliding up a panel on the side."

Les meubles fabuleux was the name of Benoit's one-man company. He built chests, bureaus and bookshelves that resembled modern sculpture. His makeshift stage was gone, as was his video equipment. That area of his loft now served as his workshop. Hung from a track on the ceiling was a heavy curtain that, when closed, encircled his benches and lathes to halt the spread of sawdust. Referring to this curtain and the one around his bed, Charlotte said, "These are the only curtain calls you get now."

As he fixed them a pot of chai tea with cardamom, she sat at a lime-green pine table and turned on her tape recorder. She claimed Dédé had been her favourite character on *Dossier criminel.* "I was so sorry you didn't show up in season two."

"I did appear," Benoit said. "For two minutes."

"Yes, Dédé went to the corner store for a pack of gum."

"And simply vanished."

"Now you see him, now you don't."

The vanishing act had been his idea. The producers had concurred, thinking he was leaving wiggle room to eventually wiggle back onto the show.

Benoit served Charlotte a cup of chai and sat beside her. "But then Dédé's dead brother reappeared, played by Dany Savard," she said. "He hadn't really been dead. It had all been a fantasy of Dédé's." With her one eye, she managed a look of incredulity.

"Hey, what can I say? The show sucks."

That got a laugh out of her.

"So that was Dédé's fantasy. What about yours?"

"This, I guess," he said, nodding toward his work

space. He meant finding a natural talent, something that didn't give him dry heaves, panic attacks and heart palpitations. When he wouldn't renew his TV contract, Mommy Wingood had yelled, "What the fuck's wrong with you?" He began mumbling some excuse, and Wingood slammed her palm on her desk: "Articulate!" He looked her in the eyes. "I hate it," he finally said, honest for the first time. "It's torture." Wingood stared at him awhile. Then she crumpled his contract into a ball and lobbed it at him. "You're free," she said.

Charlotte Dupuis wanted to know why he'd gone AWOL from showbiz. He took a sip of his chai.

"Not my cup of tea."

"Could you elaborate?"

"No."

After ten minutes of his laconic answers to questions about his former career, he changed the topic by showing her a new dresser he'd designed: an equilateral triangle, with the successive drawers growing wider toward the bottom. "At the back is a signature detail of mine." Concealed in the back panel was a drawer no larger than a soap dish. He pulled the drawer out.

"A hidden compartment?" she said.

"For valuables—jewellery, mementoes, whatever."

Soon the magazine's photographer arrived. The man

took pictures of the furniture and of Benoit leaning against his equilateral triangle. Between shots, Charlotte asked about a design award Benoit had just been nominated for. "It's called the Niche Awards," he replied. He could see the one-eyed reporter shaping this information into a headline about a former actor finally finding his niche.

"Speaking of awards," she said, "at the Gémeaux ceremony four years ago, you won the New Face award. Most winners thank everyone, from their director to their kindergarten teacher, but you didn't do that. At the podium, you pleaded with somebody to phone you."

What he'd said was: "I'm still mediocre. But please call me anyway. Please, I want to talk."

"What a dolt I was."

"You were speaking to a girl, I suppose."

Charlotte Dupuis grinned and Benoit nodded.

"I bet she called you."

"You bet wrong."

Across the room, the photographer snapped a picture of Benoit's own dresser with its blue undulating sides. At the back of the dresser was a tiny drawer Benoit hadn't opened in a long while. Its stash: a single cassette tape. The only thing of hers he'd kept.

———

In high school, Benoit had had a natural talent for gymnastics, particularly for the parallel bars. A few weeks after the "Whatever Happened To" article appeared in *Lundi*, he stopped by a community centre on the Plateau to sign up for a gymnastics class for adults. Through the aquarium windows on the ground floor, he watched the swimmers doing laps and then headed up to the second floor to locate the registration desk. He passed a gym filled with clanking barbells and then a yoga class where students were pretzelled, knees balanced on elbows. At the end of the hallway, opposite the registration office, was a window into a dance studio. In this room with mirrored walls, people in their fifties and sixties, mostly women, were flinging their arms over their heads. They shuffled in one direction; they slid back in the other.

At the front of the room, a woman with a ponytail knelt in front of a portable stereo. The music—Benoit could just discern it from behind the glass—switched to something more rhythmic. The dancers in their sweatsuits and leotards pogo-sticked twice and then, arms akimbo, skipped three steps forward.

The teacher with the ponytail stood and faced the class.

It was Madeleine.

She was blonder, slimmer. A look of deep concentration on her face. She clapped in time with the music: Slap-slap-slap. Slap-slap-slap. Slap. Slap. Slap-slap. He felt these slaps. The brutality of what she'd done years earlier. Yet as he watched her weave through the dancers, position their bodies with her hands, the sting faded.

One dancer, patting a hand towel to her forehead, swept out of the studio and bent over a drinking fountain in the hallway. Through the open door, the music blared, something jazzy with horns. Over the music came Madeleine's voice. "Slide, slide!" she cried. "Slide on over to the other side!"

The dancers slid across the floor.

Someone tapped Benoit on the shoulder: the woman who'd been at the drinking fountain. She had a glistening forehead and a child's inquisitive stare.

"Hey, didn't you use to be somebody?"

This happened a lot. Usually he owned up. Not today.

"I don't think so," he said. "But I'm starting to be."

The woman headed back into the studio. He followed. He stood in the doorway and watched a roomful of grey-haired dancers slide-slide-slide and Madeleine clap-clap-clap.

"*Scène dansante,*" Benoit whispered to himself.

These two words appeared in the final act of Madeleine's *Jaybird* script. "*Scène dansante*" was the prologue to Tchaikovsky's fantasy ballet, she'd explained. It dawned on him now, in the doorway, that a prologue was the start of something. Not the final act.

ACKNOWLEDGMENTS

I am very grateful to Lexy Bloom in New York; Michael Schellenberg, Dean Cooke, Ron Eckel, and Suzanne Brandreth in Toronto; Helen Garnons-Williams and Kelly Falconer in London; Kathrin Scheel in Frankfurt; and Brigitte Bouchard in Montreal.

Most of these stories have appeared in magazines and anthologies: "Isolettes" in *The Malahat Review, The Journey Prize Stories 16* (McClelland & Stewart) and

Coming Attractions 04 (Oberon Press); "Green Fluorescent Protein" in *Event, The Journey Prize Stories 14* and *Coming Attractions 04,* and also in Russian in *Inostrannaya Literatura;* "The B9ers" in *NFG;* "Bang Crunch" in *The Fiddlehead;* "Scrapbook" in *Maisonneuve* and *The Journey Prize Stories 17;* "The Butterfly Box" in *The Antigonish Review, Coming Attractions 04* and *Headlight;* and "Extremities" in *Lust for Life* (Véhicule Press). I'm grateful to the editors.

"Jaybird" was partly inspired by Dave St-Pierre's choreography *La pornographie des âmes.*